A Reluctant Hero

ALSO BY FRANÇOISE SAGAN

A Reluctant Hero

Françoise Sagan

Translated by Christine Donougher

E. P. DUTTON   NEW YORK

To my son Denis

*Published in the United States by E. P. Dutton, a division of
NAL Penguin Inc., 2 Park Avenue, N.Y. 10016.*

*Published simultaneously in Canada by
Fitzhenry and Whiteside Limited, Toronto.*

Originally published in France under the title De guerre lasse.
*First English-language edition published in Great Britain
under the title* Engagements of the Heart.

Library of Congress Cataloging-in-Publication Data
Sagan, Françoise, 1935–
A reluctant hero.
Translation of: De guerre lasse.
1. World War, 1939–1945—Fiction.   I. Title.
PQ2633.U74D413   1987   843'.914   87-6699

ISBN: 0-525-24550-2

COBE

10 9 8 7 6 5 4 3 2 1

First American Edition

Chapter One

THE SEASONS, too, were harsh in the year 1942. As early as the month of May, the meadows were already yielding to summer. The tall grass, softened by the heat, stooped and wilted, and broke off at ground level. Above the artificial lake, a little distance away, trailing mists hung like smoke in the evening, and the house itself, with its pink wrinkled façade, its upstairs shutters closed on some secret and its French windows, downstairs, wide open on some surprise, seemed like a slumbering old lady on the verge of a stroke brought on by uncertainties.

Yet it was after nine o'clock, and coffee had been served on the terrace at the foot of the steps in the hope of coolness; but it was so light and still so warm that one might have thought it the middle of the day and well into summer.

'And it's only May!' said Charles Sambrat in a gloomy voice. 'What shall we do in August?'

He pitched his cigarette-end ahead of him, in a brief inexorable trajectory that perhaps in his eyes presaged their future but that Alice Fayatt watched from the depths of her rocking-chair without disquiet. It was a vigorous gesture that had cast the incandescent cigarette into the void, onto the gravel. And in the twilight, the man's silhouette, his vital gesture, spoke of life far more than inexorability; the large brown eyes, full mouth, fleshy nose of Charles Sambrat – surrounded and set off as they were by astonishingly black, fine hair and eyelashes, worthy of a woman, worthy even of some Valentino – were in no way suggestive of anything disquieting or even prophetic, whatever there was of a rather old-fashioned, slightly 1900s' style of good-looking ladies' man about him. And for once, not sickening, thought Alice. The man's healthiness, his evident joy at being alive for once did not sicken her like some anachronism, or lack of awareness, shameful in this month of May 1942. His total indifference to the history of his country made her otherwise indignant, but there was a kind of accord – to think of it was exasperating, but it was undeniably there – between this man and the smell of this house and of his meadow, and the line of his poplars and hills; in short, an accord that would have lent weight to the fine tricoloured, apple-green speeches of Marshal Pétain had she been able for one moment to believe in them. And all at once, Alice thought she could hear the old man's ringing, solemn voice, then, more distantly, the harsh, yelling voice of a madman, and she blinked, threw back her head and turned instinctively to Jerome.

Jerome, too, looked as though he had been lulled by the smell of warm grass. His eyes were closed and the locks of his light hair were hard to distinguish against his tired, vulnerable, drawn face. Jerome's face: she owed him everything today, the grass, this star-studded sky and the sudden respite for her nerves; everything, even the vague but ambiguous pleasure, this vague nostalgia inspired in her by the overmasculine charm of Jerome's childhood friend, Sambrat, on whom they'd only just descended that same day with no explanation – the friendship spared them the necessity of giving any.

She blinked and shook her head to attract Jerome's

attention, before realizing that he too had been looking at her, with wide-open eyes, for a long time now. This generalized blindness towards him seemed to her proof either of her own egocentricity or of her casualness in his regard. A bird sang behind them, its voice odd, and Charles began to laugh: 'That bird's singing like a carter,' he said in a cheerful voice. 'I always have the impression it's saying rude words. Don't you think so? There's nothing romantic or pretty about its trills. There's even something furious about them that makes me laugh.'

'It's true,' said Alice, politely at first, but then with amusement – for it was not inaccurate. 'Perhaps it's a confused daytime bird, exasperated by its confusion.'

But what were they both doing here, she and Jerome? What were they doing talking about a bird's irate song with this poor young man, a shoe manufacturer by profession, in the Dauphiné?

'That was a truly awful meal I cooked for us,' Charles went on, but in a voice so devoid of concern that it sounded almost cynical.

This man must be completely impervious to embarrassment or remorse, thought Alice; and though she hated pretentiousness and even peace of mind, whether in town mice or country mice, braggarts or gay dogs, Alice could not but smile, despite herself, at the memory of Charles, dumbfounded and delighted by their arrival, dangerously cooking an unhoped-for omelette in his kitchen. That had happened an hour earlier – an hour, already! – and the echo of that laugh of his robbed her, at least for this evening, of all critical faculties. The man must quite simply be good-natured; a quality these days as anachronistic as his physical appearance. A quality that at least would serve the plans she and Jerome had. And she was sure of it; goodness was inscribed all over him – on Charles's face and in his bearing. He was a handsome young man, but also a decent one. Exactly as Jerome had said, but the condescension she remembered having noticed in Jerome's voice all of a sudden seemed unjust and ill-timed. After all, however much of a womanizer, materialist or narrow-minded blockhead he might be, thanks to his two guests, Charles Sambrat might one day find himself shot against a wall or in the hands of sadistic brutes, without even knowing why. There was no question of telling him why before knowing if it would have the same meaning for him as it did for them, and seeing him dozing here in his tranquil corner of France, she suddenly felt disgraced, the desecrator of a hospitality that was both immemorial and sacred. For a moment she felt like the wolf in the fold, until she caught the liquid, brown, staring eye of the sheep called Charles Sambrat looking at her body . . . and all at once had to renounce her wolf role.

'But don't you realize how wonderful your omelette was,' Jerome protested. 'In Paris, my poor friend, people would fight over that omelette!'

'Aren't you exaggerating a little?' said Charles, not without some irony. 'Food supplies will sort themselves out, you know,' he added, 'the Germans are frightfully organized.'

'Ah, you think so! . . .' Jerome's voice sounded distant, abstracted, hardly mocking at all.

He was already starting his investigation, thought Alice wearily. He was already beginning; could he not have waited for one more evening, just one evening away from all that? And a hundred jumpy, badly lit images passed in procession beneath her eyelids: doorways of seedy-looking hotels, dark streets, railway stations, short-stay rooms, scarcely unpacked suitcases – sad, dirty, anonymous images, sordid images, always with sharp angles, the images of the Resistance, in a word; and in this rounded meadow, beneath this vaulted sky,

[8]

with the curve of the poplars over there, these images were all the more terrifying. She felt tears welling in her eyes. They should not have come here. They should not have stopped and rested, they should have continued to run, from one streetcorner to the next, from one doorway to another, zigzagging, perhaps falling. They should never have come and stretched out on this piece of land, so peaceful, so round, in front of this man with a round neck; a neck straight and rounded like those famed birches, those necks described by a sensuous woman in her exquisite novels. That straight, suntanned neck beneath black hair that was too long; hair that belonged to an abandoned man, she thought suddenly.

'You're not married, Charles?' she asked, or rather heard herself ask, in an almost anguished voice, and blushed in the dark, furious with herself for this indiscreet question. A question Jerome had advised against the day before. And she was also just as promptly furious with herself for her idiotic and incongruous feeling of pity towards this provincial little cock-of-the-walk who was so peacefully happy with his bachelorhood, so patently sure of himself. This small-time industrialist who considered the Germans so organized and France so well fed and her own body so alluring; who thought everything was for the best in the best of all worlds.

'My wife's left me,' said Charles without looking at her. 'She's living in Lyons at present. I'm a little disorganized, but there's Louis, and his wife, Elisa, who comes and cooks throughout the week – except Sundays . . . that's why supper was so filthy. If you'd let me know in advance . . .'

'But,' Alice stammered, huddled in her chair to hide her blushes, 'surely you don't think I was talking about your omelette, I . . .'

'I know, I know,' said Charles, 'of course I know.'

And he gave a little embarrassed but encouraging laugh that made Alice's confusion total.

'Forgive me,' she said, standing up, 'I was half asleep, I was talking in a dream, I can't tell any more. The meal was actually delicious, but I must go to bed. I'm dead tired, the train journey was interminable. We were travelling for twenty-four hours, weren't we, Jerome?'

The two men had hurriedly risen, but of course Jerome got entangled in his chair, so it was Charles, tense and trembling, who got to Alice's side first, and she observed the two men – treating her as though they were all in an American comedy, she thought in a sudden burst of gaiety, and hastily turned away towards the house before she laughed.

'I'll show you to your room,' said Charles, 'or rather, no, I'll let Jerome do it, he'll be better at making you comfortable; he knows the house as well as I do, I'm pleased to say,' he said, resting his hand on Jerome's arm – Jerome having come hobbling up to them. 'But I'm sorry to say, he knows better than me what you like,' he added with unexpected, old-world charm, before making a gesture that involved taking one step back and inclining towards Alice, without taking her hand, in a dry, almost distant little bow that seemed to the young woman suddenly a great deal more erotic than the most lingering and fiery hand-kissing. And to set herself at ease, she smiled candidly at him and met his gaze – those eyes so brown, so masculine, so childlike, the eyes of an animal, in fact, devoid of the least shade of ambiguity or insolence.

It was a gaze she remembered having seen only in men looking at women: men whose path she'd crossed on beaches when very young, whose bearing, gaze, everything about them owned honestly and serenely to an unbridled desire for women, and concealed only with difficulty a boredom and total aversion towards other

[10]

men. She remembered having known two or three men like that, very calm and very handsome, very polite and very discreet, often almost retiring. Women would let themselves die or kill themselves for them, without anyone being able to blame the men for the least cruelty. These men did not mix with other men. No other vice – not sport, not cards – held any enticement. For these men the only inhabitants of this planet were women: the women they loved, then left, the women they sometimes lived off, too – calmly, without embarrassment and without greed. But this leisured species, so well described by Colette, had long since disappeared and its descendants – if there were any – surely did not manufacture shoes near a place called Romans. 'No, no,' Jerome was saying, 'no, no, it's your house, you do Alice the honours. In my opinion, she'll like the yellow, straw-coloured room. I'll come and say goodnight later, Alice,' he said in a lower voice, 'if it isn't too late.'

She smiled without replying. She allowed herself to be led away, drowsy with weariness and pleasure, surrounded by a smell of dried fruit and wax polish that she'd thought vanished from her life.

Following a taciturn and formal Charles, who strode slowly ahead of her with his hands joined behind his back like a guide or estate agent, she walked through what she took to be a drawing room – a large drawing room that had panther skins on the floor, with holes in their sides and glass eyes, and a few bright red portraits hanging askew on the walls; then a hall, then a staircase where some gun-dogs were dozing. They didn't disturb them. Then at last, she came to the threshold of a huge square bedroom with large pink flowers, pale and full-blown, fading on the walls, around a large bed, suitable for a confinement or a honeymoon and covered with a crocheted bedspread. But what she saw before anything else, and what she rushed towards, was a great fire blazing fiercely in the hearth, as though it was the middle of winter. And Alice, who liked nothing so much as a wood fire in the summer, open French windows in the winter, and long swims in lakes beneath the autumn rain, cast into the mirror over the fire an intrigued eye at her host. He had left his friends only for a few minutes after dinner – indeed, for the time needed to light this fire, and in the very room that had been recommended only at the last moment by Jerome. He watched her. She saw him standing on the threshold, saw his reflection – the reflection of that erect body, hands still joined behind his back; and saw, above all, his glance, a glance that slowly skimmed the room, the windows, the fire, the bed, the gleaming wooden floor, a proprietary glance, both critical and pleased, a glance whose expression did not change as it came to rest on her, until the moment it met her own glance in the mirror and faltered. She turned abruptly to face him, embarrassed and annoyed that he should have caught her catching him unawares, and prey to a wave of hostility and exasperation, above all, at the idea that Jerome's previous plans and amused forecasts should have turned out to be so accurate and her advice so unnecessary. Annoyed – now that, for once, she finally wanted to be useful, longed to be useful – that her own role should be of so little consequence, or the result of something for which she had so little responsibility. An old anger welled up in her, an anger long since forgotten, an old rebellion of woman-as-object. The desire of this possessive, smug petit-bourgeois, content with his furniture, his houses, his factories and his mistresses, and the glance that dared add her preemptively to these pretentious, primary possessions suddenly drove her wild. She would have hit him if he'd been closer. But as though mysteriously alerted, Charles Sambrat strode across the room without a word, opened the window, pushed back the shutters and, with his head

[12]

outside and not even turning round, exclaimed: 'It's completely idiotic, but you must see this; you know there's a full moon this evening. It's going to be splendid. Don't forget to look at it and make a wish.' He had no sooner regained the door than he added 'And get some fresh air,' as though they had all spent the evening in a cellar and not out on a terrace.

Alice Fayatt fell asleep as soon as he had gone, and she forgot his glance and the mirror and their arrival in this room. When she half-awoke in the night, she remembered only that the man was tall, with large hands, that he'd opened the shutters with an expansive gesture onto the trees, there, where the black leaves stood out against a tremulous, dark-blue sky. And that for just a second the world had reeled beneath the thrust of his hands, his voice, his laughter, his diffidence, that Alice herself had reeled simultaneously with the shutters into the Milky Way and the peaceful night, into sleep and safety. For she had been on the run, hiding with Jerome, for a year now. For a year now she had been frightened, holding her fear in contempt. And, for a moment, as she stood on the squeaky floorboards of a provincial bedroom, while the gravel crunched beneath the hairy paws of the two dogs in the dark, she had forgotten that there could be other footsteps that would make the gravel crunch at dawn, soon perhaps.

'Your girlfriend seems to like the house,' said Charles Sambrat, sitting down again in his armchair, facing Jerome – all he could see of Jerome, now that evening had fallen, his long silhouette, the gleam of his eye, and his white hands. But he knew Jerome's gangling body by heart, his hair and pale eyes, his face with its slightly too fine features. And all this made him, in Charles's eyes, a man just as ugly as any other.

'And what do you think of her?' asked Jerome.

[13]

Charles froze, astounded. Ever since the day when Charles had taken Jerome, still a virgin, to a brothel – the same week that Jerome had taken Charles, already an ignoramus, to the Louvre (but it has to be admitted that the discovery of women had a far more resounding effect on the life of the one than the discovery of painting had on the life of the other) – ever since that far-off time they had never exchanged the slightest comment on their various conquests; and Jerome especially had never sought any approval from Charles, who in any case considered his friend's girls quite pretty, but very boring. And now, after five years apart, on the very evening Jerome had brought him the most beautiful, desirable, the only possible woman in Charles's eyes, he had to go and ask his opinion! For a moment Charles wavered, about to tell him the truth, namely: 'She's for me, Alice is mine, I must have her, I want her and I love her. I want to seduce her and, worse, I want to keep her. You were mad to bring her here. Even if I have no more chance than one in a hundred, I'll try for it.'

But he was silent. Not out of patience, but superstition. For the chance that he had, that chance in a hundred – he didn't really know what it depended on. Charles, in fact, never relied on his physical appearance, despite all the successes it had obtained for him in more than fifteen years. He knew he was attractive, but this seemed to him like some sort of certificate of good health, a kind of visa that allowed him to explore a country but not to settle there. Because he found men extremely ugly, he couldn't imagine that he might be pleasing to women, except for his cheerfulness and the way he shared as equitably as possible the physical pleasures he set such great store by. All in all, there was so much modesty in his handsomeness that it was impossible to hate him. Those few women he might not desire, and the men other women belonged to, entertained no thought of holding a grudge against Charles Sambrat. Instead they would condescend slightly, display a kind of disdain or abstractedness when he spoke to them, and thus take their revenge, in the most prosaic, most discreet way possible, for the attention other women paid him. Charles Sambrat had come to think of himself as not very intelligent, or at least to think of intelligence as a lesser faculty in him; this was vaguely painful to him, like some kind of disability, one of those innocuous disabilities that other people make fun of; you accept this with a laugh of self-recognition, but it sometimes gives you an odd bruise.

This modesty of both body and mind was something Jerome was familiar with in Charles, and it was perhaps this modesty that had made him accept, and even love, the companionship of his friend.

'I think Alice is wonderful, absolutely wonderful,' Charles replied in a dull voice, but after an interval that seemed long to both men, and that made Jerome turn round vaguely in his chair, grow agitated, and suddenly remember that Alice, for all her refinement, was a woman, and women, even refined women, rarely remained indifferent to Charles.

'And how's business?' he asked all of a sudden, drawing another look of astonishment from Charles. Business had always been deeply distasteful to Jerome, or at least deeply boring. It was another one of the taboo topics of conversation between them.

'At the moment, you know, leather . . .'

He seemed to be justifying himself, and Jerome started to laugh.

'You still have doubts about how good a businessman you are, Charles, answer me! You continue to doubt your thinking ability?'

'No one's ever required any of me, you know,' said

[15]

Charles. 'Except you, perhaps, when you wanted to educate me. But that was a long time ago.'

And he lit a cigarette, looking up at Jerome, who thought he saw looking up at him in the darkness the sad, gentle eyes of a lovely, uncomprehending animal. He was momentarily touched by it. Everything that Charles had managed to say or do, even his enthusiasm in making them welcome, his good humour, his whole attitude had confirmed the description he'd given Alice in advance. Occasionally he'd seen her smile, faced with the accuracy of his sketch; to the point where Jerome had felt embarrassed by it, guilty even; stupidly, for, after all, if Charles had no demands other than those of his temperament, and no ambition other than that dictated by his own comfort, then there was nothing terribly shabby about describing him as handsome, mediocre and kind. The truth was shabby, not him, not Jerome.

'You're intelligent, Charles, but you live among nothing but cretins. How can you expect to remain intelligent? You've always had the same pals – the barmen in Lyons, the doctors here, all your pathetic card-playing, womanizing, sex-mad pals. You're just as indulgent as ever, my poor old friend.'

'And you just as condescending?' Charles asked suddenly, so quickly that Jerome was lost for words. Oddly, he had forgotten that out of his friend's mind – calm, hazy and apparently so frivolous – there could sometimes burst flashes of irony.

In any event, there could be no question of settling this problem this evening; Jerome must have Charles as a friend, he must keep him as a friend, and now as a supporter and accomplice.

'I take it back,' he said. 'I expressed myself badly. When I said "indulgent", I didn't intend anything disparaging.'

[16]

'But you were,' said Charles. 'And I, too, was disparaging. But we've always accused each other of these things. So, what the hell, let's talk about something else.'

There was a moment's silence, then Jerome started laughing – his hesitant, awkward, juvenile laughter, which Charles immediately echoed with great relief. For though he was completely indifferent to Jerome's opinion, a mad rage increased within him as the minutes passed, as he looked upon this blond-haired man, this old schoolfriend and remembered that he was shortly going to climb, confidently and inevitably, into Alice's big white bed. To touch her, kiss her, waken her. The man two metres from him, supposedly his friend. He was going to lie on top of that supple, long body; he was going to kiss those grey eyes and black hair, and that red mouth. A mouth so finely turned, perhaps for the sole purpose of damming the blood that swelled it, the blood whose ebb and flow heightened its redness and fullness.

A mouth so red that Charles knew that by pressing his own mouth to it he'd instantly feel the beating of the woman's warm blood, her salty, sugary blood, as though in the unknown, independent, maddened heart of another person. Yes, he loathed Jerome. It would have been better if he'd thrown them both out before, and not let them in, not let them cross his threshold, rather than subject himself to the nocturnal imaginings and fantasies that awaited him. It wasn't an old friendship that held him back from throwing them out at this very moment; it wasn't his upbringing either. It was the hope, the mad hope, the fatal desire of being able himself one day to join Alice in that bed beneath the crochet counterpane. If one day that were allowed him, he, Charles, wouldn't stay on a terrace muttering commonplaces with an old friend. No, he'd be up there already, bending over; bending over his double, his wife, sister, daughter, mistress – his love. He wouldn't stay here exchanging inanities with some stranger, some cripple – in a word, some male.

His desire must have been contagious, for Jerome stretched his limbs in his armchair, yawned openly, braced his knees. He was on the verge of getting up and Charles was desperately seeking some way of detaining him. Politics, of course, that's all anyone talked about! Jerome must be for or against Pétain. Given that Pétain represented the established order, he must be anti-Pétainist, that was certain.

'And what do you think of Pétain?' he asked.

Leaning back in his chair, he spoke in a listless voice, but without looking at Jerome, for fear of being caught out or having his mind read. For while Charles had not lost the desire to play the fool, neither had he lost his concern over being caught out at it. And once he was thirty, this even worried him a little. So, it was without seeing Jerome that Charles sensed him relax, withdraw his hands from the armrests on his chair, and settle back again. And while Charles congratulated himself on his guile, Jerome was congratulating himself on his patience. Now at last he was going to find out how Charles had developed.

'To tell the truth, I don't think very much of him. And you?' he asked cautiously.

'Oh, he's not so bad, he's not so bad,' said Charles, suddenly alert and talkative. 'No, no, I don't find him too bad at all. He saved us from the worst, after all.'

Jerome forced himself to breathe slowly. He had endured conversations of this kind for the past two years in Paris, just as he had heard it said for the past three or four years that perhaps, after all, Hitler was just a good German, concerned about his country; and at times he wondered whether he wasn't going to crack up one day or another, and jump at the throats of the people talking to him. For though this nonsense might be uttered out of ignorance or hypocrisy, it was uttered, above all, out of a great concern for comfort and peace of mind – and this was what infuriated him most.

'Meaning you don't think this is the worst?' he asked in a voice that he tried to control, to keep amused.

By way of reply, Charles gave a wave of the hand, indicating the meadows, the house, the hills in the distance; indicating himself, stretched out and well fed; indicating all that he had preserved intact and heartening, despite the spurts of blood splattering across Europe.

'Oh,' he said, 'we're in the Unoccupied Zone here, you know, perhaps it's very different. So what happens in the Occupied Zone that's so terrible? I've heard that these Germans are very correct?'

'True, there's sometimes one who gives up his seat for an old lady on the bus,' said Jerome, 'and everyone congratulates and compliments each other by the look in their eyes, as though they had all selected the right people to be occupied by. But meanwhile, their secret police – nothing important – the SS, the Gestapo are arresting anyone in the least bit Jewish, anyone in the least bit Communist, and sending them all off, women and children included, to camps they don't come back from.'

Jerome's voice was breathless and slightly hoarse with anger, Charles noted. There was no question but he was off on the right lines, he was going to keep Jerome with him until dawn. If he set the ball rolling again, but cautiously, and didn't throw it too far ahead, the odds were in his favour.

'When you say "don't come back from", you mean that they haven't yet come back. We'll have to wait until the end of the war, maybe. There's still England and the United States, thank God, and others who are going

[19]

to join in. Because, when all is said and done, they aren't going to spend their whole life here, after all,' said Charles, he, too, suddenly annoyed. 'Be reasonable, Jerome, they can't live in two countries at the same time. They've got their wives waiting for them, they have to produce children for the Führer. They aren't going to be endlessly dug in at Paris and Versailles, are they?'

'Well, believe it or not, that's just what I do think. They've taken a group of children from their mothers' breasts, put them in some sort of special schools, where they emerge in serried ranks to join the army, replacing their elders on the battle fields and in the occupied towns. We'll have warders, turnkeys, who will be younger and younger, but we'll have them, you can count on that. As long as there's something to loot or someone to kill in this fine country, they'll stay.'

'As far as looting goes, they do loot,' Charles admitted, for once in agreement. 'You can't imagine what I have to make shoes out of – straw, wood, scraps of rubber, old tyres – it's dreadful! On that score, my friend, I can tell you, as far as looting goes, they loot! There isn't a shred of leather left in the whole of Europe.'

There was a pause, and Jerome suddenly stood up, looking weary.

'Well then,' he said, 'you see, at last we're in agreement. We're looted by our conquerors and they're sure to leave one day, unless their children take their places! That's the programme for the future. If that's what you like, then that's what you like! And on that note, I'm going to sleep!'

'But come now!' said Charles, horrorstruck. 'Come now, we can argue a little, can't we? Don't go losing your temper like that!'

Jerome was standing in front of him, shifting from one foot to the other. He seemed tired and vaguely puzzled, and he was looking at him the way he might have looked at a complete stranger, thought Charles, and he lowered his eyes involuntarily.

'Is that what you've turned into, eh, Charles?' Jerome asked suddenly, in a youthful voice, a voice that sounded sincere for the first time since his arrival. 'Is that what you're like now, Charles? You complain about not having leather for your shoes when little children are taken to the far ends of the earth because their noses are more or less hooked. That doesn't upset you? You've come to that, have you, Charles? But you have heard of the Jewish pogroms, haven't you? And that's how little you care about the Jews?'

Charles suddenly raised his head in a fury.

'Hey, that's enough, Jerome, go easy. You know very well that for me there's no such thing as Jews, there never has been, I don't even know what it means, what the difference is. If you were to tell me that you were Jewish, that I was Jewish, I wouldn't care either way, it wouldn't make any difference, surely you know that, Jerome?'

'Perhaps,' said Jerome, 'yes, perhaps for you it's true, but for them there is a difference, do you see, a complete difference? A Jew is not a German, a Jew is not an Aryan, and therefore he has no right to live. Do you understand?'

'You're exaggerating,' said Charles automatically. 'Listen, sit down, Jerome, you're making me feel dizzy. Don't talk about such things standing there as if you're about to take off. Sit down,' he repeated bluntly. 'Sit down, for heaven's sake! We haven't seen each other for five years, you can spend five minutes talking to me! After all, you know,' he said, 'I'm a little lonely here. You know, it isn't much fun every day since Hélène left.'

He was actually beginning to be moved to self-pity and suddenly felt his heart aching before this portrait he was drawing for Jerome. It made him forget his relief

[21]

and joy at Hélène's departure, the celebrating he'd done since, driving in all the towns round about in his old car. It made him forget Lalie, and Veron's little clerk, and Madame Marquez, and finally it made him forget . . . in short, he was a heartless person. He was heartless, he was a liar, and Jerome must know this since he was laughing that spiteful, sarcastic little laugh of his. He was laughing, but he had sat down again, and, after all, that was all that mattered.

'Look here,' he said, 'look here, Charles, it's me! Hey, remember? It's me, Jerome. And what's that dumb broad Hélène doing in Lyons? Have you heard from her? If ever I saw a pest of a woman, it's her. Where the hell did you find an intellectual like that – you, Charles? Whatever came over you?'

'She cold-shouldered me,' said Charles sadly, studying his fingernails, which he would do whenever he was slightly ashamed. 'She cold-shouldered me, and I thought she was simply stunning. You know, it was at a time when I didn't really know what to do with myself – you were in Paris, I'd botched my education, your scarlet fever had prevented us from going off to the war in Spain; in short, I fell in love, or at least I thought I'd fallen in love, and that was that. And since she was the kind of girl a man marries, I married her. And since she wasn't for me, she left. And since she left, I was on my own and I played the field, but that doesn't in any way alter the fact that I'm a lonely man, Jerome, make no mistake.'

'You say lonely, and the rest of the time you think of yourself as free,' said Jerome harshly. 'It's the way you're made: you were born to be free twenty-three hours out of twenty-four, and to feel lonely for half an hour.'

'Listen,' said Charles plaintively, 'I take it you didn't come here to give me a lesson in morality. Or did you?'

'No,' said Jerome, 'you're right, I didn't come here to

[22]

give you a lesson in morality. Anyway, I'm going to bed!'

And he was getting up again, the beast, he was off again! But how irritating he was being, he really was the end! No, there was no doubt about it, they would have to stick to politics. As usual it was only politics that interested him. Charles spoke hurriedly, abruptly:

'I wasn't speaking from a moral point of view, you know that, Jerome. But do you really believe there's nothing worthwhile in Nazism?'

That was putting it rather strongly, of course, and he was aware of it, but he had no choice. It was either that – coming out with dreadful nonsense – or else spending an hour, an hour and a half – he didn't know how long his insomnia might last – imagining Jerome in Alice's arms, Alice opening her arms to Jerome, closing her arms round Jerome, kissing Jerome's cheeks, eyes, mouth. No, no, no, no, no, that was impossible.

'Nazism?' Jerome was saying from very far away, from very far away indeed. 'Nazism? Have you gone mad, Charles? Don't you know what Nazism is? Haven't we always been in agreement on that at least?'

'Well, I've been thinking,' said Charles, 'and I wonder if this theory of order, you know, and the superior race – granted it doesn't seem very democratic, but isn't it necessary, occasionally, in certain tragic times, to take tragic measures? The end doesn't justify the means, so people say, so you say, but isn't it necessary sometimes, I don't know myself . . .'

Jerome had slightly moved his head; a light reflected from the house fell on his face and he seemed even paler than before, if that were possible. He really must be very tired, he looked shattered, poor Jerome! Charles suddenly felt moved to pity. If it weren't for the wonderful Alice, the lovely Alice, the irresistible Alice, how glad he would have been to see Jerome again, to

[23]

take him off on some ridiculous jaunt – like it or not, he would have laughed – to old Madame Pierrot in Valence, or Dr Lefébure in Romans! For whatever he might say, Jerome could laugh as well, now and again, at least he used to be able to, once upon a time. But he mustn't overdo it! Jerome knew him well, they had talked politics often enough together, and together they had packed their bags for Madrid.

'Of course not,' he said 'I don't like Nazism, I hate Nazism, as you well know, Jerome, I was simply wondering whether there wasn't something good in it, something salutary at least for the Germans after years and years of poverty and famine. I was wondering whether Hitler hadn't, uh . . . helped them, from an ordinary, everyday point of view, do you see?'

'What do you call "everyday"?'

Jerome's voice, which he could barely hear any more, sounded heavy and bitter. It was the voice of a grown man, and to his great surprise Charles suddenly felt old. For the first time in his life he felt old, the same age as this thoroughly grown man, who was speaking to him of the world and of the havoc in the world, and of the importance of the world, and of responsibility. And this man tarred him with the same brush as himself, he was sure of it! Charles was sure tht Jerome thought they were both equally responsible for the disappearance of Jewish children. And yet, heavens above, God knows, he had nothing to do with it! Jerome was exasperating about that kind of thing, he was always putting Charles in hopelessly tight corners, and being an honest man, thank God, he would put himself in them too. By the time he got out of this one, rosy-fingered dawn would have broken at last and Alice would have slept alone.

Charles searched his pocket for a cigarette, lit it, and joyfully asked: 'And in the first place, how can you be sure about the Jewish children?'

And so it was that in his desire to keep Jerome away from Alice until as late as possible, Charles argued with him about political life until late into the night. And so it was that he fiercely defended, with a conviction he did not feel, both the merits of Marshal Pétain and the good breeding of the occupying forces. He was delighted and relieved to leave Jerome a little before dawn – Jerome who was amazingly upset and dejected by these very abstract reflections that, usually, coming from Charles, he wouldn't even listen to.

Chapter Two

ALICE HAD slept straight through without once waking up, as though her body, even when slumbering, had felt safe. She had woken up in the large country bedroom unhurriedly, scarcely surprised. The shutters weren't properly closed and already allowed the rays of an early sun, the sun of May 1942, to filter through onto the faded, flowered wallpaper. She could hear sounds that were different from those in town. Someone was pruning a tree in the distance, chopping away irregularly. A man with a gruff, indistinct voice was holding a conversation with a laughing woman and the hens in the farm next door cackled furiously. Only the sound of the stream somewhere on the far side of the meadow made a constant murmur. Closing her eyes, she could imagine people, their stances, their different and distinct gestures, and this was oddly restful after that muffled, roaring, anonymous ferment that Paris was steeped in.

Her hand reached out for her watch. It was ten o'clock in the morning. She had slept for twelve hours and felt well, wonderfully well. She would have liked to stay for months, years, between these rather thick sheets, in this room where the smell of yesterday's fire still lingered. But Jerome must already be waiting for her downstairs with his strange friend, the seducer of the Dauphiné.

She got up and pushed back the shutters. The terrace and its plane trees were drowsing in the sunshine. Between the poplars, the lake beyond lay glistening. The rocking chairs from the day before were still there, only a breakfast tray had replaced the cups of coffee on the pedestal table. She felt she was dying of hunger as she cast her eye over the bread, butter and jam laid out just below her. Charles was coming round the corner of the house. He raised his head as though someone had called and was treated to a beaming smile.

'Up already?' he called out.

He came and stood squarely beneath her, his hands on his hips, looking up, so obviously delighted to see her that she went on smiling at him. Besides, he was handsome, with his shirt unbuttoned on his suntanned skin, his mass of black hair gleaming in the sun, his soft brown eyes, his white teeth. He was like a very fine-looking, healthy animal; a handsome happy man – and perhaps he was indeed no more than that: a happy man. Perhaps he was even especially gifted for that, for happiness. Alice had always had an obscure admiration for these most rare of privileged beings.

'I slept very soundly,' she said. 'This house is even lovelier in the morning than in the evening.'

There was a pause. He was looking up at her, with his head thrown back, smiling, and his whole expression marked his approval of what he saw. He deliberately allowed a moment to pass, then spoke again:

'Aren't you hungry? I'll bring a tray up to you.'

'No, no,' said Alice, drawing back from the window. 'Don't bother, I'm coming down.' But she beat a hasty retreat towards the bed, where her transparent night-dress would cause her less embarrassment.

'Where's Jerome?' she called out foolishly in the direction of the window.

She got no reply. She was overcome with a mild attack

of uncontrollable laughter as she hastily climbed back into bed. Alice Fayatt at breakfast, fearful of the advances of an attentive leather-worker! She was thirty years old and the firing squad was much more likely to await her than rape. Why was she rushing for cover between the sheets like a frightened young virgin? This must be a dream!

'Here we are!' said Sambrat, coming through the door sideways, holding a huge tray in his arms. 'And that's another miracle, I didn't spill a thing! Shall I rest it on your knees? It is tea that you drink, isn't it? Or has Jerome again tried to discredit me in your eyes?'

He placed the tray on Alice's knees and perched himself on the foot of her bed, poured her tea, offered her the sugar, started to butter the slices of bread, then abruptly gave up his endeavours and took voluptuous pleasure in the lighting of a cigarette.

Alice rediscovered the exquisite joys of good tea, lots of butter and bread that was almost white. She practically forgot about the rest of the world. All she saw in Charles now was the generous donor of all these incredible delights; she ate and drank without a word, with an affable but distant expression in her eye, while Sambrat swelled with pride and pleasure, a cigarette in the corner of his mouth, like a character in a gangster film.

'You smoke like a film gangster,' she said suddenly.

He glanced at her anxiously before taking the cigarette out of his mouth, looking hurt.

'And as for you,' he said, 'you eat like a mischievous child. You've got jam on your chin, and it looks as though you might have some egg yoke on it as well.'

'No?' said Alice, horrified. And she sat up in bed, energetically rubbing her face with her napkin – to no avail – until he burst out laughing, delighted with his prank.

[29]

'But it's not true! So you're a liar as well!' she exclaimed.

'As well as what?'

And since she said nothing, feeling put out, Charles carried on himself: 'As well as being lazy, egotistical, bourgeois and a Fascist.'

'A Fascist?' she repeated, 'but why?'

'Ah! But then it's clear you haven't seen Jerome since yesterday evening,' said Charles with a little toss of the head that was full of satisfaction, of approbation even, and that somehow shocked Alice. 'I spent the whole evening, until dawn, pretending to be a Nazi and collaborator. All in order to prevent him from . . . well, from waking you. I thought it would be better if you were left to sleep in peace . . .' he mumbled, 'after the journey, the change of air.'

Alice sank back against her pillow. 'Jerome must have been furious,' she pronounced in an unruffled tone of voice. 'He has a horror of Fascists. In fact, he finds it hard to put up with those German uniforms all over the place, in Paris.'

'That would drive me mad too,' said Charles sympathetically. 'I swear to you, if I didn't have important things to do I would certainly be in the maquis, showing off with my great-uncle's blunderbuss.'

Alice looked at him, screwing up her eyes a little against the light. Charming, thought Charles fondly. More than charming.

'I see,' she said. And she rebuttered the same slice of bread for the tenth time. Forwards, backwards, to one side, then the other. 'I see . . . and what are these important things that prevent you from playing with your blunderbuss?'

'I have to run my family's factory,' he said gloomily. 'It's a factory that provides a livelihood for eighty fellows – the workers, their wives and their little cherubs, on

[30]

the one hand; and then there are the shareholders and the people in my family; and then there's me. In short it's all a matter of things that women find tiresome.'

'Because women aren't cut out for business, they're meant to talk about their babies and stay at home, is that it?' said Alice, carefully placing her slice of bread and butter, untouched, on the tray, as though she was afraid she might throw it in his face, he thought.

'Oh no, not that!' said Charles firmly, fervently even. 'On the contrary, women are meant to go out, into the streets, to please men, to drive them mad with love, to drive them mad with unhappiness. They're meant to travel by boat, train, go everywhere, make men dream. Oh no, they aren't meant to stay at home . . . I never said that!'

'Perhaps that's why your wife lives in Lyons without you?' Alice heard herself say, and at the same time she felt herself blush and raised her hand to her face as though to slap herself. 'Forgive me,' she said. 'I didn't mean to, I didn't really think . . .'

'My wife didn't enjoy being with me,' said Charles calmly. 'She's very fond of company, and of course here . . .'

He gestured vaguely towards the window, towards the undoubtedly little-frequented fields. He searched his pocket for a packet of cigarettes, took one out, tapped it against the packet, his eyes lowered all the while. But he had time in passing to catch a glimpse of Alice's pale, extremely pale, face, and to delight in it.

'I don't know what came over me,' she said in a low voice. 'I was rude and stupid. Are you very cross with me, Charles?'

And as he did not reply, but kept staring at the sheet on the bed instead, he saw a long hand, with long fingers and long, oval-shaped nails, enter his field of vision and advance towards his own hand, which was still resting

[31]

on his packet of cigarettes; and he had time too to compare the frailty of this foreign hand with the strength of his own, the white colouring of the one and the suntanned colouring of the other, before feeling the soft- ness and warmth of another skin against his own . . . for one moment. For one moment – before Jerome came into the bedroom and Alice's hand hurriedly drew away from his, in a movement so guilty that Charles was left amazed by it, amazed and bewildered – for one moment, for half a moment, before he leapt to his feet, far away from Alice, in an obvious manner, as though further to strengthen their complicity with regard to Jerome, she thought, as though to emphasize their guilty behaviour.

Oh, if this poor boy only knew how far Jerome was from getting angry over such a thing, how far removed from love – the fond battle of love – was their real battle. But no one except Jerome and she could gauge that distance. She was amazed to see Jerome's face actually turn red, a red that in him was a sign of anger or embarrassment.

'We've been chatting, about nothing,' said Charles, pointlessly and deliberately lying in her presence, drawing her into his lie and – if such a thing were possible – making her even more of an accomplice.

His efforts were futile, thought Alice, but he was pretty crafty for a provincial seducer. And the remorse she had felt a moment earlier for having contemptibly attacked his married life, the feeling of pity aroused in her by the modesty and even candour of his reactions, swiftly gave way to a fleeting and wary intuition of quite a different nature; an intuition swiftly lost, for the two men were now trying to outdo each other in silliness, slapping each other hard on the back, pretending to be country bumpkins, as in the old, rustic pre-war films.

'Well, old man,' Charles was saying, 'did you sleep well here in the countryside, were you woken up by the

[32]

sweet little birds? Was it the noise of dustbins that you missed, or could it have been purely and simply the sound of Nazi boots beneath the windows in your Boulevard Raspail? *Heil, schnump, heil, schnell, boom, boom, boom, boom. Ein, zwei, ein, zwei, ein, zwei, heil Hitler, ein, zwei, boom, boom, boom . . .'*

And he was laughing, the fool, thought Alice, laughing and even winking at her conspiratorially, as though Jerome's antipathy towards the Germans was nothing but some frivolous obsession, a minor eccentricity of the most comical kind. As for Jerome, he was whistling between his teeth, not any tune, but blowing air with the exasperated, stoical appearance of a man obliged to remain silent. He looked actually comical . . . yes, it was true, he was comical, with that long face he suddenly put on to confront the stupid, dreadful idiocies – unintended perhaps, but pitiful – of this good-for-nothing of his own age, his best friend. Oh, when all was said and done, the two simpletons were well suited to each other. Alice burst out laughing, nervously at first, then very swiftly something gave way inside her, something awakened in purely mnemonic fashion by the absurd boom-boom-booms of Charles, by the pathetic couple of German words he had uttered in a ridiculously harsh voice but whose effect was that the sun and her breakfast, these two handsome men at her feet, the greenness of the leaves at the window, the brightness of the day – all of it turned suddenly dark, forbidding, terrifying. And Alice raised her hands to her face and placed them over her mouth as though to stop herself crying out, before all at once turning over and hiding her face in her pillow.

There was silence. Alice was still laughing, but in little bursts, the way a person sobs. The two men stood motionless, their eyes fixed on her.

'Go away,' Jerome finally murmured without even

looking at Charles; and without looking at Jerome either, Charles turned and left the room.

Jerome was seated on the bed, he had his left arm round Alice's shoulders and was stroking her hair with his right hand. He was talking to her in a very low, quiet voice. Alice recognized it: it was his voice all right, a voice so calm and so used to her outbursts, the voice of a tender, attentive man, the voice of a father, a brother – which is what he'd been to her for the past two years. She admitted once again that she preferred this voice to his other one, the one that was louder, more hurried and more juvenile, the voice of Jerome her lover. It was remorse, now, and melancholy that prolonged Alice's tears.

The sun slipped slowly through its sky, passed over the tree and came to rest on Alice's right arm, the arm that lay outside the sheets and hung over the side of the bed, outside both Jerome's line of vision and his shadow as he leant over her. And she felt the dry, sharp-edged heat of the sun, she even felt, mysteriously, that this heat was yellow, golden yellow. It was fine outside and all was well. She suddenly turned, presenting her face – surely swollen and made ugly by her tears – to Jerome; but by now she was no longer ashamed to show it to him. Jerome had far more often seen her tears than heard her laughter; at least this morning he would have seen both.

'Forgive me,' she said finally. 'Forgive me,' she corrected herself, using the intimate 'tu' form of the verb this time. They had been lovers for six months, but had lived together for eighteen months without being lovers, and she sometimes forgot to use the 'tu' that Jerome set so much store by, despite the fact that she never addressed him that way in the presence of other people – or perhaps especially because of this.

[34]

'I'm the one who ought to be apologizing,' said Jerome. 'Charles is vile. Don't be angry with me. I should never have brought you here, but I didn't think he would turn into such a bastard.'

'Why a bastard?' asked Alice. 'He's crazy, or thoughtless, or incredibly tactless, but . . .'

'You don't know the things he said to me yesterday evening,' said Jerome violently. He stood up and began to pace the bedroom. 'Oh, last evening was quite enough for me, I can tell you! You know the kind of thing: the Germans will eventually go away, it's just a matter of time, anyway they're very, very correct, as everyone knows, this thing about Jews is just propaganda, and Pétain, ah yes, Pétain, I quote: "Pétain is, after all, a decent . . ." wait, let me remember . . . yes . . . "Pétain is a decent little old man, a bit of a senile specimen." What's so funny?'

'Oh my goodness,' said Alice, laughing unconstrainedly this time, ' "A decent little old man, a bit of a senile specimen!" What a thing to say! He's crazy. And you're the one who doesn't know everything. He took you for a ride yesterday! He didn't want . . . hah, hah, hah . . .' she shrieked with laughter, half overturning her tray and catching it in mid air . . . 'that Charles of yours really is a scream . . . he didn't want you to join me . . . He would have sung you the *'Horst Wessel Lied'* if you'd wanted him to . . . just to keep you longer. I can assure you, he almost confessed as much.'

Jerome's look of stupefaction increased Alice's mirth tenfold. She recovered her composure, but when Jerome, taking advantage of her silence, raised his hand as though claiming the floor at a meeting, Alice forestalled him.

'It's true,' she said. 'In any case, the first part of your plan has more than succeeded. I was supposed to seduce him, and have I seduced him! Not that it's anything to

[35]

boast about, though. The poor boy, all alone here in the country . . . the first woman to come along would have served the purpose.'

'Are you trying to be funny?' said Jerome indignantly. 'Charles all alone? Charles deprived of women? But Charles has two women, two mistresses, in the village, five kilometres away; he has three in Valence, two in Grenoble, he must have a dozen in Lyons! Don't make me laugh! And believe me, if he's been seduced, it's not for want of choice, I can assure you of that.'

'Oh well, that's all the more comforting,' said Alice calmly. 'If it's the human being he likes in me and not merely the female, we're saved. And really, it's certainly more flattering for me, after all . . .'

She stretched, extended her arm towards the window, towards the sun, drew a deep breath, then breathed out, all in a movement of pure physical joy that Jerome had never seen in her before and that made him smile. It was an anxious, uneasy smile, but one so happy to see her like this, at last, that she was suddenly still and looked at him gravely. And her grey eyes, still reddened with tears – tears of laughter, of fear – were all at once awash with tenderness; a tenderness he noticed even before she moved her arms sideways, in Jerome's direction, keeping them parallel and unbending, until she could touch him, until she could place her hands round his neck, onto the nape of his neck, and draw him against her shoulder. She said in a muffled voice: 'Oh Jerome, you love me, Jerome,' and her intonation was such that no trace of enquiry was detectable, but there was no possibility either for him to pass comment on her failure to use the *'tu'* that was so precious to him. Then he drew himself up, or she pushed him away, imperceptibly – he never knew how and when their embraces were broken.

'Come, now,' she said, 'let's be serious. Let's forget

about our Don Juan for a moment. What's the place like? Is it as convenient as you remember it?'

'Marvellous . . . Marvellous!' he said, first of all almost with regret – regret at leaving Alice's shoulder – then gradually with animation. 'Marvellous! Just imagine, the demarcation line is twenty-five minutes away, twenty-five kilometres, practically no distance at all. The train passes at the top of the hill, right at the top of a slope – in other words, it's doing five kilometres an hour at that point . . . old ladies can jump on and off as easily as goats. The next village is five kilometres away. There are eight hundred inhabitants, decent folk, on the whole, who work for Charles mostly, and like him because "he pays them well and isn't stand-offish". The police force consists of a fellow who puts in an appearance from time to time; he lives by himself on a nearby farm and rides around on a bicycle. Every three weeks he comes here on the quiet to clean Charles's silver. They drink a bottle of claret together (or two, or three) and Charles tells him everything that's been going on. The nearest small town is twenty kilometres from here – that's Romans. To get there, or send his boxes there, Charles has at his disposal a van, three lorries and his own car. Finally, the countryside is wooded, mountainous, difficult to get to know. As for people's general mental outlook in this province, I'm slightly familiar with it, having spent holidays here with Charles. They're quiet folk, a little miserly, but not malicious. And I'm pretty sure that the word "anti-Semite" means nothing to them.'

'Just imagine,' said Alice, 'just imagine the number of Jews we could get out, perhaps going through here, in this very house, then afterwards along that road, and further on along the other road, then onto the highway, and finally the road to the sea, the sea and the boats

[37]

and peace. Do you think we'll be able to do all that, Jerome? Jerome, do you think we'll manage to do that?'

'But of course,' said Jerome, laughing. 'Of course we will. What else have we done but manage for the past few years?'

'What else have *you* done, you mean,' she said. 'I certainly haven't done anything, and you know it. I've never helped anyone, I've only ever been a person who has to be helped. But you've helped everyone, all the time.'

Jerome didn't feel at all proud or arrogant about either his life or himself personally. He had always lagged behind, always been afraid of everything, always fought his fear; before jumping, he had retreated in the face of everything that terrified him. He had never had much of a natural gift for life. He was born lame, with a sceptical mind and a heart full of sadness; he had nothing but regrets and yearnings. He was born disappointed, anguished and loving. And even though he knew Alice would never deceive him, even though he knew he would always love her, even though he knew that one day this love would cause him to suffer mortal pain, he knew too that this was his destiny, and that all dreams of a happy love with a woman who dreamt of no one but him were other, different dreams, born of the sleep of another man.

He shook himself.

'Meanwhile, we're going to have to win Charles over,' he said with a smile. 'He's going to have to accept that his factory might be burnt down, his workers shot, he himself tortured, his house reduced to ashes. He's going to have to accept that he must put all that at stake if he wants to retain our high regard.'

'Or my favours,' said Alice.

'Or the hope of your favours,' Jerome corrected her. 'In short, we're going to ask everything of him and give him nothing, is that it?' said Alice. 'And do you think it will work?'

'But of course,' said Jerome. 'Men like Charles are capable of doing absolutely anything for the women who resist them. It makes their desire ten times greater. On the other hand, if the women surrender . . .'

'Surrender, surrender, what an ugly word,' said Alice, 'it's a term of defeat.'

Jerome was getting annoyed.

'But as you well know, if they're to do absolutely anything for a woman, some men need to be left unsatisfied, to feel frustrated . . .'

'Or made happy,' said Alice slowly.

And she turned away. She wore that ambiguous smile that he had occasionally seen on her face in Vienna, at those parties where he'd met her before she was really ill. That ambiguous smile that stopped men in their tracks and left them standing in her wake, following her with their eyes, their nostrils flaring as though she'd emanated a curious, unknown perfume, but one they recognized. That odd smile that had fascinated Jerome and today made him feel once again a little afraid.

'Come on,' he said, smiling and taking Alice's arm to pull her out of bed. 'Come on . . . We're beginning to bombard each other with maxims, but we didn't come to the country to play *"liaisons dangereuses"*.'

'My God, how true,' said Alice laughing. 'Have you noticed how you quickly feel ridiculous when you talk of anything other than the war. It's dreadful. Jerome, be a darling and leave me to get dressed while you go and see poor Charles, who must be beating his breast in the garden. Tell him it wasn't his boom-boom-boom that drove me to despair, that he didn't put his foot in it, that he's in no way to blame for my hysterical sobbing. Or rather, yes, on the contrary – start now! Start to tell him the beginning of my sad life story; then I will

[39]

whisper the rest to him. Run along, quickly, Jerome, but don't be vengeful on my account. I'm going to get up, get dressed and go frolicking in the meadows.'

Chapter Three

CHARLES WAS seated on the steps to his house, his dog at his feet, but not in his usual position, with arms and legs thrown out to right and left. Now he was all hunched up, arms hugging legs and chin on his knees. He was staring into the distance with the fixed expression, the look of total assurance that indecision always gave him.

Jerome came and sat on the steps as well, but a good yard from Charles, and lit a cigarette without saying anything. Charles's rounded back, the raised hairs on the nape of his neck, his grave demeanour signalled the most profound, and unusual, melancholy. Jerome nevertheless waited, sadistically, for Charles to speak first. A vague sense of rancour mingled with his feelings of pity, for after all, if the situation had been different, or rather Alice different, if Alice hadn't been such a vastly superior person to Charles and in particular to Charles's kind of love affairs – if Charles had had the least chance of seducing Alice, he would not have hesitated: he would have taken her, or tried to. 'All rights and all responsibilites,' Jerome suddenly remembered. Indeed this was the motto the two of them had written all by themselves a long time ago on that strange bible, at that uncertain age when boy-scout mottoes still have some hold but cynicism has too. And they had planned

[41]

for every event in their lives with this completely ingenuous cynicism of adolescence. One of their laws laid down, among other things, that just as the house of either was the house of the other, and no excuse was needed to move in or turn up in the middle of the night, so too was the other's woman a possession that could be gaily appropriated, if she agreed to it, and no reproaches made. This implied a sense of detachment and a moral code of conduct that were half-English, half-barbaric, and must have captivated the imagination of these virgin boys (or half-virgins, for Jerome suspected Charles at that time of having already acquitted himself quite well with the baker's daughter).

At eighteen, these decrees still ruled their lives a little, and they were neither then in much of a hurry to leave their adolescence behind; anyway, not enough to openly repudiate or burn their decrees. So they kept them. But so far, they had both naturally broken the rules; each, for instance, finding it more agreeable to be met at the station by the other whenever they visited. As for women, neither had ever felt the slightest desire for the other's inamorata, their love affairs had never been anything but relationships running parallel to one another. But now with Alice, whom he also desired, Charles was opportunely remembering the code, openly wooing her. But he appeared not to be in the best of form; in fact he seemed very low.

'Stop sighing like that,' said Jerome, 'my hair's getting blown all over the place.'

Charles turned sharply to face him.

'You aren't angry? No kidding, you aren't annoyed with me?'

He looked really anxious, thought Jerome, smiling in spite of himself. Or rather, he would have looked anxious if his colour had been different, if the whites of his eyes hadn't been so white, his face so suntanned, the taut muscles beneath his skin so hard, so developed, if his furrowed brow hadn't been hidden by such thick, shiny hair. Anxiety could do nothing but glance off that face. A face you no longer saw any more, anywhere.

For nowadays you only saw that colour, that healthiness, that animality in Hitler's young soldiers, those SS men stripped to the waist, up in their tanks. All inhabitants of the occupied countries were pale, thought Jerome. It seemed that the young soldiers in the German army had seized from Europe not only liberty, peace and life, but the sun, the wind, the sea, even the fields. But he knew that behind these thousands of young athletes, rising from out of the ruins, from the depths of cellars, from everywhere, were their counterparts – the whitish, worn-out negative versions of themselves. A people, when not doomed to barbed-wire fences, who were dedicated to darkness, to holes in the ground, to secrecy. As though each of those fine young men trained for war had, without knowing it, begotten another man of different blood, the bloodstained and ravaged reverse side of the Aryan martial coin. Among the most rebellious and violent of these men were those helping Jerome; those who, with him, helped others to survive in dismal hotels, seedy stairways, freezing bedrooms, in overcrowded trains, dark storage rooms, in the terrifying metro system, everywhere. And everywhere, gathering slowly like this, was a whole wretched army. A whole generation of men and women the world did not yet know of, but whose unimaginable existence Jerome had found out about as early as 1936. A whole new type of human being, already equipped with a new language, a language all its own, not at all the language of dictionaries. It was a new vocabulary in which the word 'daylight' amounted to 'prison cell', the verb 'run' meant 'run away', and the word 'meeting' spelt 'disaster': and finally a vocabulary in which the expression 'tomorrow'

[43]

or 'the day after tomorrow', if followed, as in peace time, by a question mark, was also followed by suspension points. It was there, there in that hellish network, that Jerome had been living for nearly five years, six years, and it was that network that Alice, in her turn, wanted to enter.

'If you're not furious with me, shall we have a drink together?' said Charles, who had paled slightly all the same, and seemed very sorrowful. 'Will you drink with me, Jerome?'

'Of course,' said Jerome.

Charles returned as quickly as he had gone. He was brandishing a bottle of very dry, chilled white wine that had a slightly fruity, strong flavour and tasted delicious to Jerome – and even more so to Charles, who swallowed two or three large glasses full without drawing breath. He had waited nobly to be forgiven before resorting to this tonic; he hadn't slipped into the kitchen to find some ready consolation, and Jerome was touched by this diffidently sought approbation – over little things, over details – that Charles had always craved of other people (while asking for none whatsoever over the things that really mattered to him). Jerome was continually redis-covering in Charles something of that gangling adolescent who was kind and straightforward, a little too much of a skirtchaser, a little too chivalrous, a brawler and at the same time gentle, lazy but alert, brave to the point of madness; the adolescent who had been his friend. He would have been a marvellous resist-ance fighter if he hadn't been so taken up with his little leather factory and the wretched Pétain. But since he wasn't thinking for himself, they were going to do his thinking for him. Jerome began to laugh to himself. 'Why are you laughing?' said Charles sternly. 'How can you laugh when she's still crying?'

'Who?' said Jerome.

[44]

'Alice!'

'But not at all. She isn't crying any more! It was nothing, just nerves; it was tiredness. Life in Paris is tiring, you know, she has a tiring life.'

'But why? But what exactly was it that I could have said to make her cry? I want to spare her that, old man, I don't want that woman to spend her holidays here with me, crying. It's out of the question! What's the word that triggered it off? Do you think it was my "boom-boom-boom-boom"?'

And he re-enacted his 'boom-boom-boom-boom', but without the high spirits of a quarter of an hour ago; it was no longer the joyous hammering sound of a regiment on the march, but the sad, crushing boom-boom-boom of an elephant about to die. 'But no,' said Jerome, 'it wasn't your boom-boom-boom, it was . . . but there again, yes, you're right, it *was* that boom-boom-boom. There's one thing you must understand, Charles: Alice's husband was called Gerhardt Fayatt; he was an extremely well-known Austrian surgeon, the best surgeon in Vienna . . .'

'And?' said Charles. 'Is he dead? What happened?'

'No,' said Jerome drily. 'He isn't dead. Although he would have been by now! No, he's in America. But he was . . . he's Jewish.'

'Ah yes,' said Charles slowly. 'Ah yes, that's right, people told me that in Austria the Germans had for the most part behaved like bastards.'

'For the most part, yes,' said Jerome, who found these understatements increasingly difficult to handle. 'For the most part. Anyway, during that same period, Alice wasn't feeling too good. They had some . . . I don't know . . . they went through a bad patch. To cut a long story short, they were divorced. He left in a state of despair and she stayed behind in a state of despair. On

[45]

top of which, she hated herself for it – herself, not him; because, frankly, he wasn't to blame.'

'Is she Jewish as well?' asked Charles.

Jerome gave him a searching look, but all he saw in Charles's eyes was a total indifference.

'I don't know,' he said. 'I don't think so. Why, would that worry you here, would that cause you any problems?'

'Me? But why should it?' said Charles. 'Are you imagining things?'

'And the people in your factory, in your part of the world, in this part of the world – I wouldn't know myself, I haven't been here for ages – aren't they anti-Semitic? Don't they read the Fascist rag *Gringoire?* Don't they listen to Marshal Pétain's speeches, and Laval's, don't they know that the Jews are a dangerous race, a race that's robbed them of their money, their potatoes and their woollen socks, if not of control of the whole of France? Don't they know all this here?'

'Oh, listen,' said Charles, 'I honestly don't believe there's a single person in Formoy who spends time reading such nonsense, or who cares to believe it. Well, what did the Germans do to Alice in Vienna?'

Jerome felt like laughing; perhaps he only needed to say that Alice had been slapped three times by an SS soldier to turn Charles into the most genuinely and fiercely convinced of partisans. But that was not what was required. It wasn't a gentleman incensed by something rather ungentlemanly that he needed. He wanted a man who knew why he was fighting, and why he was perhaps risking death. Quite simply, he needed a different Charles; yet the same man who lived right here, with this face, this intelligence and egoism. Perhaps it was, after all, a venture that had no chance of succeeding.

'Why did you go through that Pétain routine with me

yesterday?' he said with an abstracted air, and yawning a little to make quite clear how little importance he attached to the innocent farce, which had, after all, made him bellow with rage all morning in his bedroom. 'Why did you play the dimwit collaborator until four o'clock in the morning?'

Charles picked up his glass of white wine and drank slowly, with one hand raised to give himself time to lie, just as you raise your hand at poker to give yourself time to bluff. By the time he put his glass down he'd thought of something. Jerome could see it in his eyes.

'Well, it's simple,' he said laughing, 'it's very simple. I'm going to own up to something very odd: I'm growing old, yes, I'm ageing. I've been living all on my own in this house for so many days now, I was slightly depressed when you arrived, and I wanted to talk to another human being – that's all! And I talked politics because I couldn't really see what else we could have talked about; for if we'd been of the same mind we would have gone to bed when the hens were ready to roost . . . before dark, in fact.'

'But aren't there perhaps other things we could talk about, not just issues on which we have conflicting views?' said Jerome.

'You certainly don't look as if you know of many,' said Charles.

They looked at each other coldly, aggressively, then suddenly they smiled at each other. In spite of everything, an old friendship prevailed, stealing from one to the other. They felt now like pinching each other in the ribs, slapping each other on the back, grasping each other by the shoulders. An odd thing, especially for Charles, given his dislike of men.

'So, if I understand you correctly, you lied to me from beginning to end,' Jerome replied carefully. 'If that's the case, you carried your lying to an extreme. And now you're going to tell me that you're the head of a partisan cell, of a maquis unit in the Valence hills. Is that it? Or running about the fields with the Resistance, Charles? Or are you really, seriously, busy with your leather factory?'

'I'm really, seriously, busy with my leather factory,' said Charles firmly. 'And please, believe me, this isn't just some story. I'm not going to play at war with anyone, whoever they might be. It's quite out of the question that I should get involved in a war, do you hear, Jerome, out of the question!'

'But why?' Jerome was truly astonished. 'But what is it that irks you so much? You used to be mad about guns, you like taking risks, you like fighting, you . . .'

'I have no desire to kill a man . . . and even less desire to be killed by anyone,' he specified with admirable candour. 'I've no desire to see that again.'

'See what again?'

Charles stood up, took a few steps on the small terrace, kicking gravel about everywhere with the toe of his shoe, and Jerome caught the stricken look in the eyes of the gardener standing at the corner of the house – he had spent a good half-hour raking it smooth. After he had sent a few showers of pebbles flying in all directions and thereby set the hens and swans squawking frantically, Charles came back towards Jerome, who was still sitting on the steps. He stood in front of him and, with his legs set apart and his hands in his trouser pockets, he threw back his head and gazed searchingly at the sky.

'You see,' he said in a quiet voice, 'look at that sky, do you see that sky? You see those poplars over there, those meadows, those trees . . . ? Can you smell that fragrance, that sweetness . . . ? Can you imagine the seasons changing and all the different landscapes I've been able to see, ever since I was born, ever since living here especially . . . landscapes here that are all pink in autumn and then all light blue in spring, and then all those black hills in winter . . . ? Do you think this counts for nothing, for no more than a little pointed metal object shot through me? And then I'd be thrown into a grave and have brown dirty earth put between my eyes and these landscapes; it would all be closed off, and I'd be underneath and I wouldn't be able to see anything any more; nothing more of anything I've been able to see and breathe, which is still here, which still belongs to me, which I can still see. Do you understand? It's criminal, criminal, and no one has the right to make me do that.'

He looked so aggrieved, so indignant that Jerome, at first surprised by this vaguely poetic outburst, was well and truly astonished.

'But when did that occur to you? Where? When? What happened?'

Charles began to laugh. He sat down again and, having made as if to offer some to Jerome, he finished off the bottle of white wine with a resolute gesture. His brown eyes were sparkling now; they were all lit up with the alcohol, the heat and indignation.

'If I tell you what happened to me, you'll have to tell me everything about Alice. At least, everything that I mustn't do, everything that would upset her. Promise?'

'Yes, yes, yes,' said Jerome, 'of course. Go on, what happened to you?'

'Well, believe it or not, in 1940 it was just my luck to be sent with my company to the Ardennes, or rather, not the Ardennes, I was sent to near Metz. Well, to cut a long story short, we fought on until very late in the day there, until the end. I was with my patrol and on the day the armistice was signed – well, it was twenty-four hours before – we had our worst engagement ever. There were twelve of us, and only six of us got back. We came across a German tank, and as we just had our *chassepot* rifles we stayed put at the little farm where we'd

[49]

been quietly sheltering from the sun. And from there we fired at it. My God, the punishment we took! And it was idiotic, do you understand, idiotic! What could we have done under that barrage?'

'But why didn't you surrender?' said Jerome. 'What about your officer, didn't it occur to him to surrender?'

'But he'd gone!' Charles shouted angrily. 'He had gone looking for I don't know what, I don't know where. He'd told me – me, I tell you! – to take command of the patrol. Me! He'd asked us to hold the farm. So I asked the men: what do we do? They said they didn't know, so we stayed there like a bunch of imbeciles. And then at dawn they stopped and we knew it was the armistice. That's all. But for twelve hours, I thought I was going to die, that I was going to die like a fool. There I was, like a sucker, firing through my French window at that tank, telling myself I was going to die because of those old fuddyduddy generals, those officers who didn't know where to lead us. I thought I was going to die for that idiotic madman who's been yelling in German on the wireless for the past nine years and making everyone's life a misery. I thought that I, Charles Sambrat, a man who loves life, loves women and water and boats and trains and blondes and brunettes and cats and dogs and horses, a man who loves everything – I was going to die, idiotically, for some reason I didn't understand, for a reason that was of no interest to me, and just a few hours short of the armistice. That's all. Oh, I was furious!'

Jerome burst out laughing. He could imagine Charles in a rage, abusing his men, firing in all directions, playing the hero, getting down on his hands and knees, throwing grenades, coming back muttering and swearing like a trooper. He couldn't stop laughing. To his great surprise, though, Charles didn't laugh. He was even tight-lipped, and there was that suggestion of untrustworthiness and deceitfulness about him that anger

[50]

always gave him – all feelings that he didn't customarily experience gave him an air of dishonesty.

'But in the end,' said Jerome, 'you survived . . .'

'I did, yes,' said Charles, 'but not Lechat.'

'*Le chat?* What cat?'

'Lechat,' said Charles savagely. 'Lechat was a poor wretch, a little greenhorn. We spent three months getting to know each other. The poor guy worked in Montreuil. Well, his parents didn't have a penny – they were working class. And Lechat had been working all his life. He spent every night swotting till dawn, studying law. Believe it or not, Lechat wanted to be a lawyer. And because he worked, he'd done it. He'd managed to become a lawyer. He had his diploma, he got it just before he went to war. He was going to go back to Paris and he had a friend who was going to set up a practice and take him on. Lechat had escaped his background, and his parents were pleased with him, and Lechat was not displeased with himself either . . . and I tell you, he was even happy, that Lechat. And I can tell you something crazy: for those three months, he was doubly happy. Because there he was, at war, and for the first time in his life, Lechat, at last, was on holiday! So you can imagine! He would go roaming round the countryside with his mates; we'd drink red wine, we'd have fun, we'd shoot at Hun planes in the sky; and then eventually perhaps we'd surrender to someone, and then when it was all over, there you are, he would be Maître Lechat, the leading light at the Paris bar. Because what's more, he liked his profession. Lechat didn't want to make money, he just wanted to defend wretched culprits.'

'And then?' said Jerome.

'Well, I think he was the second to last to die. Believe it or not, I don't know what happened over on the other side, there was some confusion as darkness fell. I suppose they must have wanted to take the farm by stealth, I

don't know; in any case, at one point a door was blown
out, some guy rushed in and came across Lechat, who
had put his gun down while he got a little sleep. He was
a big bloke, Lechat's build, Lechat's age, a German;
he had nothing, he had . . . I don't know what
happened . . . he couldn't raise his gun, he was cornered.
He drew his knife. And Lechat came towards him. The
rest of us were away from the door, paralysed with
sleepiness; we tried to get up, we couldn't. There was a
scraping of rifle butts and everyone was shouting. And
I was the nearest and I saw Lechat and the German
hurl themselves at each other; they clasped each other,
you know, like boxers in the ring, when they daren't hit
each other any more; they clasped each other, they were
holding each other by the neck, like two kids of the same
age. They were holding each other by the neck so as not
to hurt each other too much; and at the same time, poor
devils – because they'd been taught it was the right thing
to do – at the same time, their two hands at their sides
were searching for their knives, their daggers, in the little
sheaths they wore on one side. And those two fools drew
their knives. And I tell you, Jerome – I saw those two
fools, I saw them with my own eyes – while those two
poor fools were holding each other by the neck and
hugging each other – like little children, I assure you –
they began to stab each other in the ribs, shouting
"*Non*", "*Nein*", "*Non*", one of them in French, the other
in German. And it was "no" every time not because
they were getting hurt but because they were hurting
each other, and that horrified them. I saw Lechat crying
'*Non, non*' as he plunged his dagger into the German's
heart, just as the German moaned '*Nein, nein*' as he
plunged his knife, without meaning to, into Lechat's
stomach as he fell. In short, it lasted a minute, it lasted
a hundred years. I nursed Lechat all night. And he was
in quite a lot of pain – the stomach can really hurt, you

[52]

know. And in the end I didn't give a damn at that moment whether I died or not. In the end, the long and the short of it, in the end, was that he repeated to me the only thing he'd said all night long, as he lay in the dark . . . and it had started to smell worse and worse, and it . . . Ahh . . . what a dreadful thing war is . . .'

'But what did he say to you?' asked Jerome, fascinated.

'He said: "It's a shame, though, isn't it, it's a shame, isn't it, Monsieur Sambrat, it is, isn't it?" He used to call me Monsieur Sambrat because I owned a factory – I don't know how he knew I owned a factory. He said, "Well, Monsieur Sambrat, it's a shame, isn't it, it's a great shame, it is, isn't it?" And there was I thinking of this poor boy and his dreary life, looking after his mother, providing food for his brothers and sisters, grinding away, spending all night with those big law books that he found hard to understand and racing to the municipal library whenever he had a moment to read – to read, to devour, to become somebody. But that bungled war that lasted precisely three days and served no purpose whatsoever, that war killed Lechat, and he thought it was a shame. That was all he said: "I think it's a shame, it's a shame, isn't it, it's a shame, Monsieur Sambrat". Ah shit!' said Charles.

He turned abruptly away from Jerome. He kicked a passing goose – *thwack!* – which flew six yards through the air, squawking, a spectacle that might well have made Jerome laugh, generally speaking, but that left him completely cold. He waited motionless on the steps. When Charles turned round, his face was perfectly calm and perfectly serious, looking as Jerome had rarely seen it before.

'That's why, my poor Jerome,' he said, 'do you see, that's why I don't want to get involved in your war games. Don't take me for a fool, I know full well that you're involved, you've always been an idealist. Do you remember, you nearly got me into the war in Spain, and what's more, if you hadn't come down with scarlet fever we would have gone. But don't count on getting me into anything like that again. The Germans will be gone sooner or later. Don't worry, the Americans will come and drive them out – or the Russians, or the English – we'll wait. We'll wait until they go. At least, *I* shall wait until they go. I'm not going to grapple with any young chap from Munich or wherever, who will have been sent here God knows why, without himself knowing why, a young chap whose stomach I'm supposed to stick my knife into, shouting "*Non, non*" while he shouts "*Nein, nein*". That's all over, as far as I'm concerned. I'm not a child any more, I'm a man. Men don't like dirty tricks like that, not men like me, at least. For silly games like that, my friend, to play silly games like that, you need a more intelligent chap than me; or someone more stupid – I don't know, you choose. But not a fellow like me, not like me.'

And he sat down next to Jerome as though exhausted by his long speech. And indeed, it was the longest monologue Jerome had ever heard him deliver in all the time he'd known him. And Jerome had to admit, though he didn't like to, that it was the most interesting.

Chapter Four

THE ONLY inn in Formoy was the *Lapin Moderne*, in the church square. Charles lunched there every day, with Conte, the stout village doctor, and Flavier, the innkeeper himself. Honoré Flavier would have liked to retain the hotel's original name – *L'Hôtel Moderne* – when he bought it, but his wife was absolutely set upon giving it the name *Le Lapin Agile*, The Nimble Rabbit. He had given way and started painting the sign. His wife had then stupidly got herself run over in the street and, at first because of his grief, then out of habit, he had forgotten about his sign. This *Lapin Moderne*, then, offered its patrons good honest fare, and no frills, but as regards modernity, it offered nothing at all. The walls were crumbling and only a few stray tourists came to stay there.

That day was the day trout was served, one of Charles's favourite meals, but the doctor and innkeeper seemed nonetheless astounded to see him arriving dead on time.

'What are you doing here?' asked the doctor, who was seventy years old and had a greater recollection of Charles's past escapades than Charles himself. He had followed the progress of Charles and Jerome since they were small and readily adopted a paternal attitude towards them that Charles appreciated. 'Are you here for lunch?' he said.

'I'm here for lunch,' said Charles, laconic as usual. 'A pastis, please, Flavier.'

'Pastis doesn't agree with you,' said Conte reproachfully, but Charles's resolute air checked him; he was obviously in a bad mood. 'And what about your guests?' Conte went on. 'Yes, Jerome and that woman. Old Louis mentioned them to Madame Clayet, who mentioned them to Jules, who mentioned them to his wife, and his wife mentioned them to mine, and so on. How's Jerome?'

'He's well,' said Charles soberly. 'Come and have a drink with us one evening, tomorrow or the day after.'

'Why are you lunching here, then?'

'To leave them on their own,' shouted Charles in exasperation. 'There are people who like being on their own, you see?'

Flavier, who was bringing their glasses, set them down, laughing his loud drunkard's laugh, and gave each of the two men a little tap on the back that pitched them, chin foremost, across the table. 'What's this, boys?' said Flavier laughing. 'Arguing, are you? Is it true, Charles, that you have a vamp staying with you?'

'It's Jerome who's got her,' Charles barked.

'Well, poor Jerome!' said Conte. 'And do you like her? Is she pretty?'

'Not bad, not bad,' admitted Charles. Having gulped down his pastis, he was signalling to Flavier behind the doctor's back to fetch him another.

'Well, poor Jerome,' Conte went on, 'he's rapidly going to find himself without a woman, don't you think? Is there still the same understanding between you two?'

'Well, you know,' said Charles, relaxing a little, 'you know, it may be that she'll turn me down. I'm afraid she will.'

Pastis had always had a devastating effect on him

[56]

and, having downed the second just as quickly, Charles all of a sudden felt quite limp, quite mellow, quite drunk. He'd had a dreadful morning. After Alice's tears, his grumbling had eventually provoked his secretary to tears, and certainly provoked the tears of Brigitte, his current companion, whom he had refused to talk to on the telephone. He had even tackled some tedious old accounts again, to the great astonishment of the whole office, and, on masochistic impulse, had telephoned home to say that he had too much work to come back for lunch. This, it must be added, he had regretted immediately. And so he had come here to this old terrace, its wooden furniture with flaking green paint and its regular bit-part players. Jerome was right: he wasn't an intellectual, he was boorish and petit-bour-geois. his job was uninteresting and so were his mistresses and his amusements; for him, having a really good time meant going to Paris and playing the swank in nightclubs, flashing about and squandering the money he got for his shoes. Jerome was absolutely right, yes, he really was. Everything about it lacked grandeur, it lacked what they, as schoolchildren or students, had always sought. A half-dead *bon viveur*, that's what he was! In fact, the only thing of the slightest good in his life, the only 'higher thing' he was capable of doing 'higher things' for was (since the day before) that woman's face. A face that was honest and absolute in its beauty and grace. He sprang to his feet and stared at the bewildered Conte and Flavier, who already had their forks poised in the air, and whose eyes until then had been fixed on the plates of golden trout before them.

'What's the matter?' said Conte, 'the trout not to your liking?'

'And what if she leaves?' said Charles dreamily.

'The trout? I'd be amazed,' said Conte.

'I'm a fool! Perhaps she's going to leave tomorrow,'

Charles went on. 'Perhaps she's even left already . . . ? After all, I'm not to know. I'm a fool, I'm sorry, excuse me,' he said, rushing for the door and leaving his two friends still clutching their forks, prongs held upright like some symbol of their uncomprehending stupefaction.

He made an alarming though spectacular arrival on his own poor terrace, which had only just been raked smooth, and braking at the last moment, he nearly ran over an inattentive peacock, causing it to shed its haughtiness and a few feathers. Elisa emerged from the kitchen wringing her hands, and set her bird to rights, while Jerome and Alice appeared at the French windows, looking startled. These three dumbfounded, dismayed faces seemed to Charles the height of the farcical – Alice of course escaping it slightly, but only marginally. He was already laughing in spite of himself as he entered the drawing room.

'Well, now, ' he said, 'what if you're as quick off the mark when the SS arrive!'

He tried to stifle his mindless fit of uncontrollable laughter and not look at them, but Jerome caught hold of him as he walked past and looked down at him, face to face. And it was then that the thought 'This cretin isn't going to kiss me, is he?' sprang from Charles's overheated imagination, while Jerome slowly – very, very slowly, it seemed to him – straightened up again.

'But you've been drinking,' he said to Charles in a cold voice, and the doctor-like aspect of his tone of voice – precise and stern – finished Charles off.

'Yes, indeed,' he said, 'yes, indeed, I've been drinking.'

And he collapsed onto a divan, in the grip of a real paroxysm of laughter, on the verge of heart failure, it seemed to him, right on the verge of it. He had never laughed like that before, or not for a very long time. My God, that voice, that voice and gesture, that anxious

[58]

face bowed over him, the very nearly disgusted verdict of Jerome's – Jerome being a stranger to all that kind of thing, far, far removed from it . . . Phew! He must calm down, he was exhausted, he was going to choke to death, his heart was surely going to burst, his ribs were contracting and causing him pain, he must stop laughing! And Alice, what must Alice think! Ah! never mind about Alice, never mind about Jerome, or himself, never mind about the SS, or Marshal Pétain, or De Gueslin, never mind about anybody at all! A moment like this was worth everything else, it justified a whole lifetime, yes, a whole lifetime; all the earth's catastrophes were justified, glorified, all anguish, all dramas, all deaths were insignificant, they were of no importance any more. Everything was going very well, everything was perfect, and had no reality whatsoever if you gave the matter a little thought; in any case, nothing prevailed in the face of Jerome's few words: 'But you've been drinking.' Especially since there'd been no suggestion of interrogation or exclamation in his tone, nor even severity; there was just a full stop, a full stop and no more. A cold full stop, one which ought to have been final in its coldness. Only, only . . . oh, my God, he was at it again, how foolish, but he was behaving like such a fool! How could he have thought Jerome was intent on kissing him? What madness! But what a mad idea! Jerome, with his clean-shaven cheeks, in his polo-neck shirt, throwing his arms round Charles's neck, in front of Alice! Jerome, kindly Jerome, dear Jerome, how could he possibly have wanted to kiss him? When he had smelt Charles, even sniffed at him, subtly, before discovering the awful truth: 'But . . . you've been drinking.' Oh, my God, he must think of something else, but he was enjoying himself too much.

'Say it again, Jerome,' he groaned feebly, sitting up again and half-opening his tear-filled eyes – he could feel the tears rolling down his cheeks, he must look ridiculous . . . but he really didn't care.

He wiped his face with his sleeve – 'on the elbow, the way children do,' noted Alice, who had been swept along by the force of his uncontrollable laughter, unable to withstand it for long. While even Jerome smiled kindly at them – without much spirit, but without reserve – as though they were two sick people.

Lunch was nearly over; they had enjoyed themselves. Alice was peeling an apple and as he watched her long neck, her narrow wrists, her long fingers, Charles was envious of the blade of the knife and the skin of the apple. He was still a tiny bit drunk, but very happy, and he had difficulty evading the desire to stretch out his hand and seize those long, nimble fingers, those painted nails, and hold them in his own.

Jerome was recounting one of their past escapades with that cool humour of his, and Charles was laughing. When he laughed, Charles Sambrat would throw back his head, exposing the swollen veins in his neck, and his jet-black hair round his ears seemed so luxuriant and so silky, the teeth in his half-open mouth so white – even the slightly chipped one on the side – his virility and healthiness so evident, that anyone at all sensitive to the joy of being alive was delivered a kind of blow to the heart. Charles Sambrat made people envious; he must have given them desires both clear and ill-defined. To women he must have given the desire to lie down and men the desire to get up, but to everyone the desire to move, to move towards someone. Alice realized all this as she daintily munched her apple, nibbling at it like a squirrel. In this sunshine her black hair suddenly seemed even blacker and her grey eyes even greyer. She looked childlike, delicate and cheerful. The two men would glance at her now and then, casting equally protective

[60]

looks over her – a look sensual in Charles's case and in Jerome's nostalgic.

Jerome was reliving his first meeting with Alice, he was seeing again the face – so lovely, so desperate, so delicate – that had straight away seduced him. Alice then, when he met her, was floundering in a deep, grievous depression incomprehensible to anyone but himself – to Jerome, who had all too often in his youth been choked with despair, despondency and loneliness to be surprised by it; to deny that beauty, wealth, love and health might sometimes be dead letters in a person's life, might even increase their feelings of shame, derision and absurdity – feelings that accompany these unaccountable fits of despair. From that evening he had decided to help Alice, to help her live, or live again; he had divided his life between her and other appalling victims that he gradually found out about. Alice, in her turn, wanted to fight the demons released by Hitler. But even if she was now cured, Alice had passed through the insatiable, unsurpassable horror of hating oneself, and thought herself no longer vulnerable to any knocks other than those that were self-inflicted, could imagine no torturer other than herself; and in this she was mistaken. Gerhardt, her ex-husband, and a few of their friends who were among the first victims of Nazism, had all too amply convinced Jerome of the opposite. Already as early as 1933, throughout the whole of Europe, efficient torturers were appearing from all sides; this Gerhardt knew, but Jerome nevertheless had trouble in persuading him to leave for New York. Despite their recent divorce, Gerhardt didn't want to be separated from Alice. In the end, once Jerome had persuaded him, Gerhardt had left, before some 'booted Aryan' made him pay dearly for being neither booted nor Aryan; only he had made Jerome promise to look after his wife, his ex-wife, and Jerome didn't feel he

[61]

had the right to throw Alice into this infernal network – he couldn't after what she had already endured.

'Charles,' said Jerome suddenly, in a neutral tone of voice, 'if I drop you off at the factory, will you lend me your car this afternoon?'

'Yes,' said Charles just as quickly, 'yes, if you lend me Alice.' And as they both stared at him, he added, 'I sorted everything out at the factory in an hour; I must say, I'm feeling quite pleased with myself. So, if Alice agrees, I can take her cycling, wherever she likes, this afternoon. We could go and swim in the Laurens. Do you like swimming, Alice? It's very hot, isn't it? Wouldn't you like to go swimming?'

'It's a mountain stream,' Jerome said in a touristy voice, for the benefit of Alice, who was looking at him. 'It's a freezing-cold mountain stream, but the water is unbelievably clear. You have to jump in and get out straight away, but you'll love the place.'

'Well,' said Alice, 'since I should love it . . .'

'Then it's true, you'll come?' Charles looked at Alice with an air of wonder, smiling weakly as though unable to believe his luck. Alice couldn't remember a man over seventeen, or perhaps even twelve, who had ever looked at her in that way.

'Yes, of course,' she said. 'What's more, I can swim, so you won't even have to rescue me!'

'I promise to bring her back to you intact,' Charles vowed to Jerome, an impulsive declaration that would have bothered no one if he hadn't stopped dead on that word 'intact' and stammered in a distressed voice: 'I mean "unharmed",' an amendment that this time set Alice giggling uncontrollably and made her dive under the table after her napkin, which was, in fact, on her knees, just where it was supposed to be.

But Jerome didn't so much as bat an eyelid, and Charles lit a cigarette with immeasurable deliberation,

[62]

until Alice resurfaced, her hair slightly out of place, red-faced with laughter and making a show of dabbing her mouth with that wayward napkin. A distraught Charles was already getting to his feet, when: 'But you'll have a coffee, won't you?' Jerome enquired amiably, sounding like the master of the house, and Charles, looking sheepish, gratefully accepted, as though he were the guest and Jerome the owner of this table. Anyway, as far as Charles was concerned, there was only one possession on earth that interested him now, and that was Alice. And towards Jerome he hoped to prove the most treacherous of hosts.

Once Elisa had lent her bike, which had no crossbar, to the 'young lady', and the young lady in question had managed, after zigzagging about for a bit, to master her mount, Charles had only to shoot along with her for five kilometres, as far as the Laurens. It was a raging mountain stream, so clear, so white that it was a relief to see reflections in it, blue or yellow depending on the light; a mountain stream that came plummeting down straight from the Vercors, but rested, or rather gathered itself for a moment here and there in a few natural pools surrounded by rocks, and then gushed forth in even greater force. It was to one of these pools that Charles took Alice, swimming pools almost, where, when young, Jerome and Charles had brought along the same young girls. But that afternoon there was no longer the least memory of a face, of the cry of a young girl being tickled, for Charles to forget. He saw and heard no one but Alice; and he examined the place that was yet so familiar to him with the freshest of critical sensibility, noted its drawbacks with an almost malevolent eye; but though there was more shrubbery, weeds, mosses, branches on either side, it was still the same slope that took you down to the water, where it at once became deep. And there

[63]

were still those long flat stones that the sun beat down upon from early to late afternoon, where you could warm yourself after bathing.

They got undressed, each of them behind a different tree; and although Charles was in his bathing trunks in no time, he waited patiently, turning his back on Alice's tree and fixing his eyes on the water – that water so clear at the edge, so dark at the bottom, so symbolic of his noble soul and base instincts. He waited for a long while before Alice came noiselessly up behind him, but he sensed her presence and looked briefly over his shoulder, giving her a quick glance that was intended to be as reassuring as it was indifferent. Alice was wrapped up in the huge bath towel that she had brought in her saddlebag and it covered her shoulders, the top of her body as well as her legs.

'What do you think of my stream? It's a lovely spot here, isn't it?'

'Delightful,' said Alice's voice behind him. 'Whatever you do, don't turn round, Charles, I look hideous. I'm thin and white. It's awful to expose oneself from head to toe in the sunshine like this, it's loathsome.'

'Not at all!' said Charles, turning squarely to face her. 'I assure you it isn't . . .'

'Please, turn round!' she begged him. 'You have a suntan, which means you're dressed. But I feel naked and ugly. Don't look at me, whatever you do. I feel ashamed of myself.'

'But that will pass,' said Charles, returning to the contemplation of his pool. 'That will pass,' he vowed fervently. 'If you want, I can go and lie down on the other side of those bushes over there. You'll be completely hidden, quite invisible.'

'Oh, that would be kind of you,' she said in a tearful voice.

And Charles walked through the thicket, grazing himself on the brambles and swearing under his breath.

'I've made it,' he shouted. 'I can't see you at all. Oh, what fun it is going swimming with you . . .'

'I'm dreadfully sorry,' shouted Alice. 'But I wasn't to know . . . anyhow, I had no idea . . . pale, I'm deathly pale, and bony . . . that's the truth of it.'

So she had no idea of the shape and colour of her body, thought Charles, much taken with the idea. Well, really, what a wretched lover poor Jerome must be . . . The women Charles held in his arms left his embrace feeling sure of themselves, sure of being desirable and skilled in love – even if they were neither of these things, or not any more. Quite apart from any physical desire, Charles had always had a great deal of affection for women, and many of his love affairs that Jerome put down to lack of taste depended rather on his kindness getting the better of him; because (and this was one reason for his popularity) he liked to feel – and he always did – a genuine gratitude 'afterwards', a gratitude that had sometimes even brought back into the beds of his mistresses their astonished husbands, men perplexed and in the end more flattered than enraged at having been cuckolded by the handsome Sambrat. In any case, he was now sure, poor Jerome deserved his misfortune, or would deserve it, or would have deserved it, sooner or later. Charles buried his head in his arms and tried to think of something else.

That man is really charming, thought Alice, removing her bath towel millimetre by millimetre behind the acacia shrub. She considered herself a little less hideous lying down than she had been just now, standing trembling in the shade of her tree. She knew that she had once been beautiful, that doubtless she still was, but this beauty had become an abstract notion to her. By dint of hating and despising her own face in the mirror, she had now developed a horror of her whole body, and it was only in the last three months that she could slip into her bath without a sense of repugnance. Of course, Jerome thought her beautiful, but Jerome loved her, and his love was so violent and had for such a long time been kept to a platonic level by her that despite her lover's passion for her she could not see in his embraces anything other than the tangible manifestation of his feelings – of their feelings, rather, for after all she loved no man alive if not Jerome; there was no one but him who could put her mind at ease, no one but him whose absence made her sad. And Alice did not imagine – actually, not a soul she knew imagined – that a woman of feeling could live with a man, and of her own free will make love to him, without truly loving him. Unless it was one of those melodramatically physical passions described in novels, but Alice knew that this was irrelevant in her case. Oddly, Jerome was too mindful of her pleasure, too concerned about her reactions, still too sympathetic to the tormented heart and mind he had nursed for so long, for her body (the wild animal body she knew she had once possessed and that had for so long been quiet) to be able to take the slightest interest in the way they disported themselves. And if it wasn't passion, if there was no constraint, who or what other than love could be making her share this man's life and his bed – this man whom she had a high regard for, what's more? She could find no answer to this, for there was none. Because it was inconceivable that a woman, out of sheer horror of herself, should allow herself to be worshipped by a man who was not her husband, and inconceivable that it might be morbid anxiety that drove her into what any bourgeois person would call a life of sin. And it was also inconceivable that Alice should not feel guilty about her body's apathy and silence whenever this man took her in his arms – a man who was virile, ardent, and so concerned to make her share his pleasure. Alas! thought Alice, she no longer loved anyone in that way, perhaps she was no longer capable of it.

At night sometimes, yes, she confessed to herself, she would have given anything for Jerome not to be the person she had needed so much, for months and months, during the day. For him to stop being so devoted to her, in short. A vulgar and indecent female rose up within her when he asked her certain questions couched in supplicatory form; she could not remember having endured this female's demands nor her desires, and she would bite her arm and wrist in fury and shame, as though the arm and wrist belonged to someone other than herself. She was unaware that her blue bruises were solely responsible for restoring Jerome's hope the next day. They were – so he believed – the only evidence in her of some obscure, confused pleasure, a pleasure violent enough to make her bite herself – that's to say, stifle with her hand or her arm the cry that he had perhaps not heard.

On the other hand, Alice liked sleeping next to that long body with skin a little too soft for a man, and with so little hair on it. She liked the feel and warmth of Jerome; she liked his hair, his voice; she liked his limpid eyes, the sometimes childish, sometimes old-man air about him; she liked that absolute goodness she saw in his eyes, and also that resignation to the love he felt for her. Alice felt at ease with Jerome; he never made her feel ashamed, or afraid, or hurt, he never failed her. And she said to herself, as you grew older, that's all you could expect of anyone else; and on reflection, it was even an incredible demand to make on anyone.

It was astonishingly hot, the sun was scorching, so much that you dared not turn your back to it. Both of them had therefore turned over and presented their faces to it, both lying in the same position, as though crucified, with their arms and legs away from their bodies, seemingly attached by invisible shackles to the ground that smelt of dust and grass and hot earth. They lay head to head, without knowing it, separated only by this bank of green and fragrant acacias. But Charles, who ordinarily would have crept round the field in order to get a good look at his conquest, was not even thinking of any such thing. If fact, he was actually feeling exhausted by the Ricards, his emotions, the bike ride and this absurd situation. His heart was thumping, a line of sweat trickled behind the nape of his neck, then coursed down his neck and shoulder, immediately followed by another trickle. Blotches of colour came and went beneath his eyelids – yellow and red, red and yellow, and then red, and then yellow – depending on whether he made his eyelids press more or less heavily on his eyes. With his hair plastered to his forehead by perspiration, and his eyes closed, he felt himself drifting, inert but attentive, attentive to the earth's surface, to the surface of his skin, to the surface of his consciousness; he was like some blind animal, roasted, happy – for he did feel oddly happy. From Alice's silence and his own came the certainty, the unquestionable intuition of their accord. This wasn't the false, blind – because vital – certainty of a despairing lover; it was the cold, quasi-mathematical, abstract certainty of the inspired gambler.

Of course, this wasn't the first time that Charles had had a presentiment, but it was certainly the first time he had paid so much attention to it and given it so much credit. The idea disturbed him and, wanting to give himself a shake, morally and physically, he jumped to his feet, raced towards the freezing cold water and plunged in. He experienced a succession of feelings: that a fist was striking him in the solar plexus, that a thousand piranhas were falling upon him to nibble away at him and that he was being thrown, all trussed up, into a flaming oven. So, after two vigorous strokes, he leapt out of the water with a muffled groan, almost as quickly as he had gone in, trembling with delayed shock. 'Jerome was right, the water's far too cold. It could kill you.'

Though groping his way blindly, he had landed at Alice's feet, but he didn't even see her. His teeth were chattering, he even had the impression that his blood was racing round his body at top speed, sometimes burning hot, sometimes freezing cold, and he was bent double, shivering, feeling himself turn blue, literally blue, but nevertheless without being able really to understand the significance of his colour.

'My God!' said Alice. 'My God, Charles, but you're crazy. That water's freezing. You're trembling, sit down!'

He offered no resistance and made a gesture of relief as he sat down on the warm grass, while Alice, with her towel in her hands, energetically rubbed his shoulders, head, chest and legs. His whole body was diligently massaged and rubbed down by the long soft hands, hands that he'd dreamed about, and whose touch he couldn't even appreciate now, being in the throes of this internal trembling, this brutal semi-blackout that he didn't know the cause of. Was it the Ricards, the water, the heat or his age? This idea suddenly made him feel like whimpering, like resting his wet head against Alice's shoulder – she looked so warm, so soft – and telling her, whining all the while, that this stream in spring was really too impossibly cold for a human being . . .

'My God!' Alice was saying. 'You gave me such a fright! And the very idea of diving into the water like that – you should have dipped your toe in first!'

'If I'd dipped my toe in,' said Charles, 'I'd never have gone in.'

[69]

'That's exactly what I mean,' Alice replied sensibly. 'Exactly that. You're crazy, Charles. Now stay in the sun a little and relax.'

She had apparently forgotten her sharp bones and livid skin. Looking after him, cajoling him had completely overcome her apprehensions, or rather given her a maternal role that allowed her to forget her role as bathing beauty. And before she changed her mind, he hurriedly stretched out beside her, put his hands on the back of his neck and closed his eyes, delighted.

He looked at her through his eyelashes, with his old hunter's look, but it lacked conviction, for the hunter wasn't in him, and if the quarry was already in the bag, *he* for once was the quarry. He was well aware of this, he had suspected as much; he already loved to distraction Alice's shoulders, which were actually broad, but thin, and her breasts, the long line of her upper body and then that tiny waist and those narrow hips, the long legs and the long neck. Everything about her was so long . . . Charles was reminded of that strange animal the giraffe, whose existence he had learned of at school, and whose shape had always enchanted him. Was it Lamarck or Darwin – he didn't know any more – but one of them maintained that the giraffe's awkward gait and long neck were due to its love of food, to a desire for certain leaves that tasted delicious but grew too high up in the trees, and this had forced the animal to stretch its once squat neck hopelessly towards them. As for Alice, she also had the most dainty, most lovely hands and feet, elbows and knees in the world, and these she'd had from birth. And he could also see, even through the prudish jersey swimsuit, the straight line of her ilium, his favourite bone in women; the bone that defined the hip on either side, and against which he would come and rest his head after lovemaking. And as he lay dreamy and motionless on this beach, with the woman's hand

[70]

playing in his hair without her having to move, and he himself halfway between the two poles, the two most fiery zones of her body, he would feel – most provisionally, but most profoundly – the owner and slave of it.

They remained silent for a moment, but the acacia bushes no longer concealed them, and they felt the want of them – oddly, each as much as the other – as of a third party who's a nuisance, but valuable, in front of whom a man and woman can hint at so much more than they would dare say openly if they were alone.

'Would you like a cigarette?' asked Charles. 'I'm going to fetch some, but I warn you, they're dark tobacco, rather strong.'

'Yes, I'd like one,' said Alice with her eyes closed.

She followed Charles's silhouette with her eyes, and watched him stroll away calmly, as though he were completely dressed. This physical ease, this assurance that was so much the opposite of his obliviousness of his handsomeness, gave rise to a touch of envy in Alice. The slightest conceit in Charles would have seemed to her the height of grotesqueness, as indeed the slightest complex would have seemed the height of absurdity. He walked like one of those very young and very handsome adolescent boys she had seen on Italian beaches, who looked as detached and unconcerned as possible about their handsomeness, but who you could tell, from their litheness or nonchalance, took intense pleasure in their muscles, their reflexes, in the supple and swift machinery of their bodies. Bodies till now solitary and happy to be so, and whose future power they were still unaware of. There was a kind of innocence in Charles, far removed though he was from chastity. He was already returning, smiling. He sat down next to Alice and lit two cigarettes. He held one out to her, looking her full in the face for the first time since their arrival in this pastoral place. And this look was so approving, so pleased with what

[71]

he saw, that rather than being made to feel uneasy or embarrassed, she felt she had recovered her serenity. She took a drag on her cigarette, filled her palate and throat with the strong bitter smoke – but it wasn't unpleasant, which surprised her – and at once expelled it from her mouth.

'I haven't smoked for two years,' she said. 'You soon pick it up again.'

'It's like cycling,' said Charles. And he too took a long drag that he swallowed with the utmost pleasure.

Really, he was a kind of sensor screen, a chameleon, a barometer of sensations and delights. Something in him registered whether it was hot or cold, whether the air was fragrant, or the wine good. It was an engaging characteristic. Alice shook her head. All that she was there for was to persuade Charles to turn his peaceful home into a forbidden relay post, his factory into a hide-out and his spare-time activities into subversive missions. Well, that would be difficult, especially in this rural holiday atmosphere that seemed to veer between the atmosphere of the Comtesse de Ségur's writings and that of *Lady Chatterley's Lover*, but in any case radiated peace. She was searching for a roundabout way of broaching the subject, a way into it, but as though mysteriously tipped off, Charles got there before her.

'I'd like to apologize for this morning, for that "boom-boom-boom",' he said.

But as with Jerome that morning, his boom-boom-boom was so lugubrious and woeful that Alice was bewildered. He had to add. 'You know, the boom-boom-boom of German boots in the streets at night.'

'You've no need to apologize,' said Alice brusquely. 'I was the one who behaved absurdly, I . . .'

Charles interrupted her.

'I didn't have any idea that you were Jewish – you or your husband, I don't remember exactly what Jerome told me – but I assure you that even so, I didn't think . . . I didn't know that it would upset you so much.' He had spoken very quickly and only looked up when he'd finished speaking. Alice was staring at him with eyes that were slightly bigger than usual, more from surprise than resentment, it seemed to him.

'You couldn't have guessed,' she said slowly, looking at him intently. 'Fayatt is an English-sounding name, but Gerhardt Fayatt, my husband – that's to say my ex-husband – is in fact Jewish.'

'I imagine that caused you a lot of problems?' said Charles. 'We don't know anything in this country,' he went on with a bitterness that was quite new in him.

'It was particularly awful for Gerhardt,' said Alice. She was waiting for him to ask her a direct question about her own origins, as Jerome had deliberately left this unclear in order to be able to gauge Charles's reactions. But he didn't say a word.

'He was the best surgeon in Vienna, in Europe, I believe. His father and grandfather had been great surgeons too, and to some extent they were little lords of Austria. Fortunately for us, the Nazis knew this and as a few of their dignitaries had health problems, we weren't rounded up in the very first month, nor deported, as three-quarters of our Jewish friends were.'

'They deport women as well?' Charles asked incredulously.

'Yes, both women and children,' said Alice, and as he was staring at her with that blank look you still got from some people in Europe – the English, for instance, or certain Frenchmen such as Charles living in out-of-the-way places, in remote provinces; in fact, all those who had not experienced occupation – she added: 'They even deport babes-in-arms, I've seen them with my own eyes.' She had spoken in a curt voice, the voice she habitually adopted to deliver these two sentences, which she always delivered together, one after the other. For though they were equally true, the second prevented anyone, no matter who, from questioning the first, however dreadful it might be, or at least in front of her. But obviously children were of no interest to Charles.

'So those bastards really take women, do they? How did you escape them?'

And since he still hadn't asked her the main question, despite the ten openings she'd given him, because all of a sudden it seemed possible that she might at last have come across a man for whom the word 'Jew' carried no more weight than the word 'brown-haired', because it seemed that for this man the supposition that she might be Jewish did not in any way influence his attraction towards her, Alice decided to tell him.

'First of all, because they needed Gerhardt, and then because in Vienna in the first instance they only took Jewish women. Not women married to Jews. Well, I'm Catholic by birth, so to speak.'

'Oh good!' said Charles. 'So then you're not Jewish!' He nodded his head approvingly, in a way that was beginning to scare Alice, then he threw her a satisfied, confiding glance. 'I didn't want to say so,' he told her, looking relieved, 'but I like it better that way. Honestly . . .'

There was silence for a second. Alice felt her blood ebbing back to her heart, and anger thrumming in her veins, at her wrists and temples. She kept her eyes lowered, but this was in order to search the ground for a stick, a stone, no matter what, with which to strike such a rotten, hypocritical man, this spurious 'good sort'. She must get back, she said to herself, and quickly. She slowly got to her feet and heard her own voice calmly asking (when she actually felt close to screaming): 'You don't say . . . And why do you like it better that way?'

'Well,' said Charles, 'because that means you're in

less danger! I shouldn't like it at all if they were to pack you off to their camps, and anyway I wouldn't let them,' he said forcefully. 'I can assure you of that. Good God!' he added abruptly. 'You're pale, Alice. Sit down. Those bastards must have really frightened you. I'd like to kill them . . .'

Alice sank down onto the ground again and hid her face in her hands for a moment, astonished by the pleasure and relief it was now her turn to experience. After all, she would have hated Charles to be hateful, and it surprised her to feel this about a man she had known for twenty-four hours. She brought her hands down to find Charles's worried eyes fixed on her, and suddenly felt ashamed of what she'd been capable of thinking.

'Forgive me,' she said. 'It's dreadful, but when you said . . . well, when you said you liked it better that way – that I wasn't Jewish, I mean – I thought you were one of those people who . . .'

'Who what?' asked Charles. 'Anti-Semites? But Alice, you must be joking? The very idea! You know, my father was a fool, but I had a very intelligent uncle, the one who died two years ago, the one I took over from at the factory. One day he talked to me about this. He explained that ever since we've been able to trace back our history a little, since Charlemagne, everyone, famous or not – Louis XIV's descendant, for instance – has had at least twenty million forebears, they must have, automatically, not to mention the unknown primitive peoples and all the monkeys before them. And he told me that if anyone could assure me that in all the migrations and movements of population there wasn't among those twenty million forebears a great-great-grandmother of his who'd been seduced by a Jew, or a great-great-grandfather who'd married a young Jewess, "if anyone can swear he's Aryan, my dear Charles, you

[75]

give him a kick in the pants for that man's a cretin.'' I thought he was right; don't you think so? This notion of anti-Semitism seems crazy to me.'

'It may be crazy, but it's real,' said Alice, lying on her back again, and closing her eyes, while Charles rested on his elbow and stretched out beside her, keeping a respectful distance. He was chewing a blade of grass as his eyes wandered over the water, and over the trees. When he returned his gaze to Alice, she had opened her eyes and was looking back at him. A certain liquid was welling up from her pupils, gathering at the outside edge of her eye, and trickling very slowly down her temples. It took Charles a moment to realize that this unexpected drop was called a tear, and to be thrown into confusion by it. He instinctively sought Alice's hand, which she yielded to him, and he placed a warm tender mouth upon it that wasn't in the least bit suggestive. It was certainly the first time she had ever seen a half-naked man in bathing trunks kissing the hand of a woman on the verge of tears.

But far from feeling the absurdity of this little scenario, she felt only its sweetness. Jerome's project, their scheming and plotting suddenly seemed to her shocking, unjust, indecent. It was out of the question now that they should tear away this affectionate, sensitive man from his pleasures, his high spirits, his daily sensual delights. She would in her turn have to convince Jerome of this, she told herself, getting up again and slowly dusting herself. But she already knew that her rebellion was only momentary, and that Charles, like the others, would just have to come between torturers and their victims of tomorrow. And he would have to even if his skin was coppery, even if his hair was silky, even if he was open-hearted, and even if she herself was actually beginning to feel a kind of fondness for him.

*

So, once they had dressed again, and discovered that the rear wheel on Alice's bike was completely useless – for Charles had decided to employ one of the good old ruses when he went to fetch his cigarettes – it was quite unsuspectingly and even with a vague sense of confusion and a certain pleasure that she sat on the handlebars of Charles's bike and, throughout the five kilometres that separated them from home, felt him bury his face in her hair, which was blown about by the wind rushing past as they cycled. And she even felt him lean his body into her back when he braced himself on his pedals, perhaps needlessly energetically. The countryside, like their cheeks, was rosy when they reached the house. And Jerome's sarcastic remarks on their cycling misadventure unjustly irritated Alice. She wasn't to know that the punctured-tyre trick had been a favourite with both boys at the time of those excited, innocent flirtations of their madcap youth.

Chapter Five

THAT SAME evening, a little later on, she was in front of her mirror and for once looking with pleasure at the reflection of her face – already turning golden, still red – beneath her blue-black mass of hair. She noted her healthy appearance, the alert expression and mocking look in the eye of the woman in front of her, the woman so conspicuously desired and shown such obvious respect by the handsome Charles Sambrat; the simple-minded, sensitive, blundering, affectionate Charles, whom she knew nothing at all about only the day before and whom today she knew almost 'by heart' – and in this instance the childish expression seemed appropriate.

She was wearing a pleated skirt, a skirt with black and white stripes, an iron-grey blouse and bluish white-gold necklace and earrings. She considered herself elegant again, without having tried to be, but without having deliberately given up being so. Jerome knocked on her door and came straight in. Beneath an obstinate brow he had lips that were too tightly drawn, eyes that were too cold, and his eyebrows were too lightly coloured to be intimidating.

The ill-humour in his face was unusual and Alice at once tried to dispel it.

'What did you do this afternoon?' she asked with feigned concern – and was annoyed at herself for her feigning.

'I visited two farms. One was empty and the other inhabited by its owner, an old fellow called Gélot, who taught us to fish in the old days. Since he lost an arm in the 1914–18 war, he's harboured some resentment against the "Boches", as he calls them, a very strong resentment. He'll hide whoever we want him to hide, however and whenever we like ... Then I spoke to Charles's foreman – I also used to know him well. If they have papers, he'll find places for our "passengers" and even some completely plausible jobs for them. On the sole condition that Charles authorizes his employees to "play the fool", as he puts it.'

'I think he's on course,' she said smiling and looking Jerome in the face (for the first time since he'd come back, she told herself).

Jerome in turn began to laugh, but it was a strange laugh – the kind of laugh that could be described as 'yellow', where Charles's laugh was red, was Alice's sudden idiotic and irrelevant thought. She was discovering more and more frequently these mental jumps that had disappeared since her breakdown, the 'major breakdown', the shifts in tone that had so quickly established her as one of the most amusing, most courted young women in Paris and Vienna. There had been something odd, unfettered and comical about her gaiety at that time, a blend of cold humour and heated imagination, together with devastating parodies of certain individuals.

Jerome's laugh, however, was not mirthful and stopped abruptly. They both stared at each other, like two strangers – and yet they had gazed earnestly at each other a hundred times, a thousand times in the past three years, she with a questioning look, with an intense

[80]

fear of living, and he with attentiveness and matchless tenderness. But this was no longer the case; they were now looking at each other the way people defy one another. This must be stopped, thought Alice. Something dreadful was happening that had to be checked as quickly as possible.

'I'm quite sure that you've seduced Charles,' he said with false worldliness. 'The punctured-tyre trick is a sign of a truly serious attraction where he's concerned.'

'What do you mean?' said Alice.

Her voice sounded abstracted, but she had turned stock-still in front of her mirror, with lipstick in one hand, a hand that was brandished in the air and yet inert at the same time, like a film close-up arrested in mid-reel, a hand that only Jerome's reply could set in motion again.

'When we first began to go after girls,' said Jerome, 'Charles and I were just at the awkward age and our successes weren't terribly conspicuous, so we used to help Venus along in countless ways; a puncture, for instance, was supposed to throw the young ladies into confusion. We would bring them back on our own bikes, we'd smell their hair, brush against their backs. It always had an indisputable effect, at least on us . . . Of course, it wasn't very refined courting, but . . .'

'No!' exclaimed Alice, her eyes shining. 'No! Don't tell me that Charles cycled all the way up that hill with my additional fifty kilos on his bike for the sole pleasure of "smelling my hair", as you put it. That's really too touching.'

'It's no doubt touching in a young boy of seventeen,' said Jerome sarcastically, 'but in a man of thirty . . .'

'But even more so!' said Alice. 'First of all, at thirty Charles is less athletic than he was at seventeen. What's more, now that he's a grown man, and a grown man with women all over him, I give him a lot more credit for it than I would to our ignorant virgin pursuing a dream. No, no, my dear Jerome, I consider your fine industrialist Charles Sambrat quite heroic.'

And as Jerome was opening his mouth to give her a stern reply, apparently insensitive to her humour, Alice suddenly recalled an old, less innocent tactic, which she remembered as being of the utmost cunning: the boomerang accusation.

'Really, Jerome!' she said in an indignant voice, 'you aren't going to tell me that you're jealous of Charles, that you're accusing me of flirting with him? But honestly, who do you take me for? Really and truly, who do you think I am?'

There was even a melodramatic note in her voice that did not displease her. This old Machiavellianism – redirecting the accusation on the accuser, and in short, accusing him of having made an accusation – again seemed to her inspired. Alas, these subtleties were beyond Jerome.

'But yes,' he said, 'yes, I am jealous of Charles. When I saw you both arriving on that bicycle, so close to each other, looking so cheerful and happy . . .'

Virtuous indignation having failed, Alice instinctively resorted to another technique.

'But you used to say that, more than anything else, you wanted to see me looking cheerful and happy,' she said.

'Well, I was wrong,' said Jerome coldly. 'Yes, I hoped you would be cheerful and happy, but with me. Not with Charles or some other man.'

The egotism and cruelty of his remark were at once apparent to him. Alice had with a single stroke of her hairbrush brought her mass of hair over her face and he could make out neither her expression, nor even the tears perhaps in her eyes. There was silence.

'I don't understand. I don't understand you, Jerome,'

Alice's voice said at last from behind the black curtain of hair. 'You gave me the job of persuading your friend, and therefore of seducing him, didn't you? It was you who decided everything, you who brought me here, wasn't it? And sent me into the depths of the forest with a man who has a reputation for being a womanizer. Didn't you? And even if he did naively puncture my tyre in order to be able to smell my hair, that seems a trifling matter compared with the risks you were making me take by letting me go with him! I think you're being totally unfair – unfair and ungrateful.'

And tossing her hair back, she rapidly left the room before Jerome could determine the presence or absence of any tears. She was right, he was foolish and hateful and mean, and he felt furious with himself. He berated himself for a good quarter of an hour before joining them in the drawing room, still feeling ashamed of himself. Being a man of intellect, Jerome ultimately gave no credit to his impressions, instincts, fears and dreads. He believed only in his intelligence, in his reason, and this had always cost him dear.

Alice and Charles were seated in front of the fire, playing gin-rummy. In the aftermath of their row Alice's laughter first set Jerome's mind at rest, but then quickly refuelled his anger.

But what on earth was happening to him? He had just been through ten dreadful minutes; the memory of his words and foolish accusations caused him a mixture of shame and remorse. And at that moment he would have given anything at all for Alice not to have been upset and for him not to have hurt her – for him the uttermost horror. And now there was her laughter, her reassuring laughter, the very proof that she hadn't been upset, and he would have given everything in his possession in order to find her in tears somewhere, and to be able to console her himself. Indeed, he couldn't bear Alice to be laughing while they were still on bad terms.

'You don't look very well, Jerome,' said Alice, turning towards him and calmly observing him as though nothing had happened.

Hastily he lowered his eyelids so that she should not see the look in his eyes, which must be that of a madman or a person suffering mental illness.

They continued their game without getting any more alarmed about his pallor, and Alice's laughter now rang out every three minutes in response to the silly things Charles was saying. Charles, for that matter, didn't know what he was doing any more. This redoubtable player, renowned throughout the Dauphiné and the Alps for his cool and nerve at card games was playing like a four-year-old child – and not a particularly gifted child for his age at that. He was of course losing, but he didn't care because Alice was laughing, and Charles knew, or thought, that in order to seduce a woman you first had to make her laugh. This technique is actually effective, but his physique might have spared him from pursuing it. Nevertheless, he had made up some ludicrous character for himself, who always cut a sorry figure in his stories, a character who got himself rejected and spurned by women, and thrashed by men, and was always the blockhead on duty. This gave him a kind of odd charm, for there was something irresistible about the contrast between his physical appearance and his supposed lucklessness.

So Alice was laughing, she was stretching like a cat in front of the fire, lying full length on the carpet, taking off her shoes as though she was in the country house where she'd lived all her childhood. Jerome, who was used to seeing her burying herself in her room, walking along corridors with the timorousness of a maltreated dog, was astounded by this air of a contented, idolent cat, of a cat enjoying itself, a cat that wanted to go out and come home again – of a happy cat, in short. He had never seen her like this. And he couldn't believe that this house, with its pseudo-rustic or pseudo-period furniture that had been accumulated with unquestionable bad taste by Charles's parents, grandparents and great-grandparents, could in any way whatsoever seem like a cocoon to Alice. It was a terrible, sometimes impressive jumble of curios, a jumble that might perhaps have a charm of its own for anyone who had known it as a child, as he and Charles had, and for whom it would therefore have the charms of memory; but there was no way it could possibly have the charm of novelty or a charm born of the present. Yet Alice was rapidly changing since this morning. Alice was no longer afraid. She didn't come knocking on his door any more, just as she didn't come to lean on his shoulder any more, or to hold his hand; to hold it in her own slightly trembling hand, clutching him from time to time the way a person clutches a beam, or a piece of wood, when drowning. Alice was no longer afraid of the war and didn't speak of it any more. Alice had changed tremendously, in a single day. Could twenty-four hours in the countryside transform a sensitive, frightened woman, a woman who was secretive, gentle and affectionate? Could they change her into another woman who was even more secretive, but bold, cheerful, ironic and independent? No, it wasn't this house, and it wasn't Charles Sambrat either, Jerome now told himself resolutely, over and over again; in spite of everything, in spite of his own instinctive jealousy – a purely male jealousy, moreover – it wasn't Charles who could change Alice. He could at best please her and take her one evening, somewhere else, and even at some later date, but in any event not with Jerome under his roof. Alice would never stand for that, out of respect for him. Nor indeed in a field, because Alice was not the kind of woman to be made love to in a field. So he was not in any danger; he was not in any danger except that of not having Alice's attention. And this attention she would recover by herself, as soon as they were immersed once again in the conflict, in the dark nocturnal fighting, in the drains and tunnels that constituted the Resistance, and into which, he now knew, he should take her with him; not for his sake, but for hers, so that she might again become what she was and what she ought to be, what she had been during the three years he had been in love with her – as he was today, perhaps more than ever. He must take her away, he would protect her from everything. Except herself . . . naturally, but after all, he had saved her from herself once already. Jerome had saved Alice from sadness; why should he not save her from frivolity?

Jerome was forgetting one thing: that even as a child he had known this sadness, this pain of living that he had cured Alice of; and if it's easier to cure the disorders one's familiar with, it's far more difficult to cure the others. Jerome had never been frivolous, carefree, or maddened with desire for life. Gladness was just a word to him, a word in a book, whereas before Alice fell ill, she had been first a little girl then a young woman enamoured of life. She had known the enthusiasms and crazy joys, the incomprehensible feelings of euphoria that life sometimes heaps upon a human being. And Jerome could no more recognize these privileged instants in their moment of passing than Alice could avoid them. Similarly, someone blind from birth is able to understand a person who happens to become blind, and indeed is able to help him endure his blindness, but if this casualty were to regain his sight, the congenitally blind man would be unable to prevent him from leaping to his feet and running towards the sun.

'Good God,' said Charles. 'Blitz!' He broke off what he'd been saying and looked towards the door. It was one of his dogs that had come in from outside; it was limping and looking doleful, and came trotting over to him. In a flash Charles abandoned his cards, and Alice, and Jerome, and the whole of existence in order to attend to his dog. He made it lie on its back, took hold of its paw and felt it with his fingertips until the dog moaned a little, all the while singing to him in a kind of chant.

'Now, what have you done to yourself, you big silly thing? You poor fool, wait, there, there . . . does that hurt, there? No. A bit further up? Ah, yes there.'

And he said to the dog: 'Yes, that's it, that's where it is, my poor old friend. Wait. You've been running through the thickets again, haven't you? That's clever of you! That's bright! Oh, sorry, it isn't a thorn, it's a . . .

'What's this? Some sort of nail . . . so you're putting nails in your paws now? As if they were old tyres? Really! Really, Blitz, my old friend, Blitz, you must be careful! Wait a minute! Just a second! One second!'

Charles drew a little Swiss knife from his pocket – 'Just like a boy scout,' thought Jerome – and pulled out a little pair of tweezers, or something similar. He leant over the dog, but the dog yelped so distressingly that Alice jumped up and rushed over to them.

'Hold his paws, hold his hind paws,' said Charles briefly, in a tone of authority one would not have suspected in him. And Alice took the dog's trembling thighs and held them tightly in her hands. She saw Charles lean over, get hold of a little black thing in the dog's pink and black paw, and pull it out with a quick tug. The dog wriggled free and leapt to its feet. It bolted

[87]

for the door, then returned in shame and rested its head first on Charles's knees, then on Alice's, just for a moment, before going off again.

'That dog has got it exactly right,' said Jerome in a sarcastic tone of voice. 'Master first, then nurse. He might have given me a small tip, as the assistant.'

'You've never liked animals,' said Charles, sounding surly.

'But I do like animals,' said Jerome, 'only I prefer people. I distrust people who prefer animals.'

'That doesn't apply to me,' said Charles laughing.

And his laughter eased the tension.

'And yet,' Charles concluded, his eyes on Jerome, 'and yet with that English-looking face of yours, you should be mad about animals! Shouldn't he, Alice?'

'It's never occurred to me that Jerome looked like an Englishman,' said Alice smiling. 'But talking of England, Charles, can you get *Radio-Londres* from here?'

'*Radio-Londres?* But of course! All the French draw their lined curtains and sit down side by side round the family table, on the dot, in order to listen to the French addressing the French. No one thinks of seances now and of calling up the dead, it's the living who are called up, it's so much more cheerful! As you well know, of course!'

'Alas, I'm not so sure of that!' said Jerome.

'But I swear it's true!' Charles was laughing now. 'It's only the real Resistance people who don't listen to *Radio-Londres*, they have to be careful! Spend an evening in our village, for instance, when people have their shutters open because of the heat, and you won't hear anything else! Meanwhile,' he added, 'my wireless is in the library and that's where we'll be, on the dot. Do you listen to it every evening?'

'Whenever I can, yes,' said Jerome. 'But this evening it's absolutely essential that I do, there might be a

[88]

message for us. We might hear something that concerns us. In any case, I shall listen, even if you go on with your gin-rummy . . .'

But his slightly acid remark passed unnoticed.

Chapter Six

So at the appointed hour they were all three gathered round the crackling wireless that emitted the voices of free men talking of a free country. Charles was in his armchair, slightly stiff and aching after his cycling feats of that afternoon; he was watching Alice's silhouette, now close, now distant. He was smoking an old cigar that had also been discovered in the cellar, and felt time dragging a little, as he did every evening, while that same voice, which sounded so young, coming from such a distance, sent its little crazy poetic messages – messages that his guests this evening seemed to find indifferent fare, thank God. So he was stunned to see Jerome suddenly on his feet, looking white as he had never before seen him. The voice from the wireless, sounding not in the least concerned, was calmly repeating: 'The shepherds have gone and the flock is waiting. The shepherds have gone and the flock is waiting. I repeat: the shepherds have gone and the flock is waiting ... The dove has cast its net over the trees. The dove ...'

But for Jerome it was evidently not a matter of doves. He just stood there, and Alice too was on her feet, next to him. She had returned to him; and evidently, for her, Charles no longer existed. A kind of nausea that stemmed not from jealousy but from a feeling of rejection took a stranglehold on him, as he in turn got to his feet, slowly, politely, as though the 'Marseillaise' had suddenly been played, if not at the wrong moment, then unexpectedly, while he was drinking coffee at the end of a meal.

'Good God! Good God!' murmured Jerome. 'Did you hear that, Alice? Did you hear that too?'

'Yes,' said Alice in just as quiet a voice.

She sank back very slowly into her armchair, with her hands to her face, while Jerome turned his back on her, taking up a position in front of the fire and delivering violent punches to the marble mantelpiece.

'They did say . . .' he said, directing the question at himself, 'they did say: "The flock, the shepherds . . . " ' And without waiting for Alice or anyone else to reply, he suddenly turned to face a motionless Charles, who was staring at him in amazement! For Jerome's pale, fine-featured, distinguished-looking face – a face that was actually slightly weak, in Charles's opinion – had turned brutal as well as deathly pale. Charles was reluctantly discovering that Jerome's clenched jaw, the harshness in his eyes and his sunken cheeks made him look handsome. He was handsome in anger, he was handsome in action; perhaps he was even handsome in bed, Charles was already thinking with the bitterness of a cheated man. But Jerome's hand, which had seized hold of his jacket, was shaking him with a vigour Charles had not suspected in him either.

'Listen to me, Charles, you must lend me your car. I have to make a phone call, but not from here. It'll take me an hour, perhaps two. Alice, you stay here. I'm trusting you to look after her, Charles; if I'm not back in five hours forget about me for a while. I'm trusting you to look after her, Charles. But I'll be here well before then.'

And catching the keys that Charles threw him, he departed from the room. The car left immediately.

[92]

And no sooner had the engine noise departed into the night than the crickets resumed their concert of sound. Alice was gazing into the fire. Her face too had a distant, slightly sad expression.

'Can you explain to me . . . ?' Charles began very gently.

'Yes,' said Alice, looking at him without even seeing him, he noted with distress. 'Yes, I can explain. That sentence you heard means that three members of the network have been captured and are in German hands, perhaps at this very moment they've been tortured or shot, I don't know. They were friends, friends of Jerome, and then friends of mine too, for a little. And it also means,' she went on more slowly, as though expressing the thought as it came to her, 'it means that all the Jews or non-Jews waiting for us, for Jerome or me – people they know and trust, and they trust no one else – are in danger of going out to keep the rendezvous and finding no one there. They're in danger of panicking and getting caught. It means that if anyone other than Jerome or myself fixes a new rendezvous for them, they'll think it's a trap and they won't go. And since Jerome can't go back to Paris any more because they must be looking for him everywhere by now, it means . . . it means that . . . that I'm going there myself. Yes, yes, that's what it means. I must go to Paris myself, at once, tomorrow at least. The police don't know me, nor do the Gestapo. I've never done anything, I won't be taking any risks,' she added, smiling a little because he had turned white.

To her great surprise he began to shout:

'Because you think you're going to go in his place, you think that's your role? You think that Jerome's going to send a woman off to get caught, butchered and killed by those maniacs? If Jerome does that, he's mad, he's a bastard! I've already told you, Alice, for me, the role of women is to live, to be beautiful, and young, like you,

[93]

Alice. Alice . . . Men don't send their women to be killed in their place. I'd kill Jerome if he let you go! I wouldn't stand for it, Alice, you shan't go to Paris in his place!'

They stared at each other. They weren't friends at all any more, they were two strangers. A man and a woman.

'Listen, Charles,' she said. 'I shall have quite enough trouble convincing Jerome. It's six months now that he's been refusing to make use of me. But in this case, I know where the rendezvous is, and I know when it is. And believe me, Charles, whether he likes it or not, and whether you like it or not, I shall go. It's not that I'm in the least bit heroic, but there's no danger. And what's more, there are women, children and men waiting for someone to lead them away and prevent their extermination. It's quite simple, believe me. Believe me.' And she began to laugh. 'Believe me, for once I can look after someone other than myself, for once I can be of some use and help instead of being helped, for once instead of wrecking the life of a man who's in love with me, I can prevent the deaths of strangers – believe me, Charles, and don't try to argue me out of it. I'm going to wait in my room until Jerome gets back. Forgive me, Charles,' she said from the threshold, while he stood there, dazed, stunned, his cheeks flushed, his hands clenched on the mantelpiece, looking distraught and furious.

For a moment Alice realized that, roused to anger for a good reason, Charles Sambrat must be either a very dangerous adversary or a valuable ally. For the past twenty-four hours now, Alice had been watching this seducer whom she was supposed to seduce develop before her very eyes. For twenty-four hours she had been watching, with an aesthetic pleasure devoid of all sensuality, this nice boy who was rather too handsome and too much of a womanizer. This was the first moment she ceased to regard him as an actor in some ludicrous, old-fashioned vaudeville sketch, but as someone who might well perhaps be a fellow-combatant. So she couldn't understand why, as she stood on the threshold on the point of departing, she felt overcome and overwhelmed by a wave of desire that was fierce, indecent and so sharply defined that she reeled as she left the room, she too with cheeks burning.

When Jerome returned three hours later in the middle of the night, he found Charles Sambrat standing at the door waiting for him. They had a long discussion, interspersed sometimes with insults, sometimes with words of affection. In any case, when Alice came downstairs the next day she came upon Jerome, who told her, plainly and distinctly, that the part of the mistress of a manufacturer in the leather business who was going up to Paris on behalf of an engineer was, actually, an ideal cover for an untried partisan such as she and that he, Jerome, would be indebted and grateful to Charles if he accompanied her to Paris and brought her back again. Charles said nothing. He listened to Jerome. He didn't even look at Alice, but a kind of halo emanated from him, a kind of vibration in the air that was familiar to Alice, that she remembered having already noticed round hundreds of people, and sometimes experienced herself, a halo like the sun at Austerlitz, the pale and dazzling trail of happiness.

Chapter Seven

THE JOURNEY on a crowded train had been exhausting and Paris itself, where they finally arrived in the evening, in the rain, had seemed to Charles dark and dismal, echoing only with the footsteps of German patrols. Even his hotel in the rue de Rivoli, which he had always seen as having an eighteenth-century aspect to it, semi-luxurious, semi-dissolute, seemed to him today gloomy and passé, indeed positively old-fashioned. Perhaps Jerome was right, after all, in wanting to hasten the departure of these Huns. Nevertheless, adultery remaining quite obviously the best possible cover for a would-be partisan, Charles had booked two adjoining rooms, for Alice and himself, that looked out over the Tuileries. And on this first morning the radiant sun that had returned to the Tuileries Gardens, the softness in the air, and this gentle breeze that you didn't find anywhere else had restored to Charles the summery Paris that he loved so much, with its terraces, its endless days, its warm blue evenings, its empty avenues, trees and statues – all that was conducive to his pleasures and daydreams.

This evening he would take Alice to see *his* Paris; this evening he would try to listen to her, to talk to her, to entertain her, to 'divert' her; divert her from the war, the Jews, from Jerome and her past, and even from herself. This evening he would conceal his desire; he would offer her everything and ask for nothing. This was perhaps the first time Charles Sambrat had contemplated an evening of this kind, for he had always concerned himself more with the pleasure of women than with their happiness. Perhaps because he considered himself more capable of giving and sharing the former than the latter – and furthermore, because courtesy and sensuality, social graces and instinct (for once in harmony) always led him to confuse the two. It had taken Alice to make the appalling difference between them become tangible again. 'It's not just that I find her attractive, but I could love her,' he realized, and his jubilation gave way in turn to terror, incredulity, excitement. Was he about to play truant on his usual feelings – a truancy that was absurd at his age? Was he about to return to the glorious landscapes of love – landscapes forgotten since puberty, so he thought? Was he about to be rejuvenated – or become senile?

He dressed carefully, putting on one of his expensive alpaca suits, which he had bought just before the war, and which was therefore practically new, slightly fitted at the waist, and earned him a quick smiling glance from Alice when she opened the door, a glance he in his enthusiasm interpreted as admiring. If Alice had until now taken him for a country bumpkin, well, he was going to show her!

'Did you sleep well?' he asked.

He crossed the room, and went and cast a disenchanted eye over the Tuileries Gardens before turning round.

'My God . . . but you look beautiful,' he said, his voice altered.

For Alice, who was standing against the light when she opened the door, now had the light shining on her, and in this Alice, so far removed from the Alice who wore a skirt and shawl in the Dauphiné, Charles discovered another woman. She was wearing a thin, pale-yellow silk dress, and more make-up as well; she looked older and more desirable. Her mouth was redder, her eyes more elongated, her body more visible. And it suddenly struck Charles that he was in the bedroom of Jerome's mistress, and that Jerome wasn't there. His eyes met Alice's; she picked up her bag and got to the door with the least possible naturalness.

'Do you like my dress?' she said. 'It's a Grès dress, I think . . . or a Heim. It's very thin, and very, very comfortable, especially in this heat,' she went on apologetically, as though justifying her bare arms, her bared neck and the near-bareness of her whole body in that dress. 'Are you going out, Charles?'

With a new-found assurance, for he was outside the bedroom now, Charles replied: *'We're* going out. You don't imagine that I'm going to leave you on your own in Paris, in that dress and with that colouring of yours . . . You look very well, you know, you got a tan while you were staying at the house.'

He was talking off the top of his head, he was stammering, but he looked so enraptured with life that Alice allowed herself to be won over by his enthusiasm. She took in good part the ridiculous silent-comedy routine he went through with the concierge as he returned the two keys; she even enjoyed the pantomime performance of discretion and resignation in his face and voice when he replied to the hotel employee's unspoken, tendentious query: 'Yes, we're keeping both rooms this evening.'

He was very sweet, she thought in a rush of tenderness, even in that odd suit that made him look like a riding instructor who had come into money. He'd look marvellous if he were well dressed, in tweed, brown and black like his eyes, to match his skin, or in a very straight-cut dinner jacket that would show off his slimness, the straightness of his body, the way he held his head. It seemed to her that Charles entered rooms and left them, whereas other men simply slipped in and out. She was amazed to be feeling not at all frightened about the rendezvous that she had arranged that same morning, a rendezous that would perhaps lead her into a trap; after all, nothing was ever safe in these circumstances. But Charles's presence made the idea of any danger absurd. Their visit was to be delightful and his confidence that it would be so – a confidence that he made quite plain – proved infectious.

He took her to lunch in a smart restaurant, known in the past for being very chic, but where the food was now dreadful; for Charles, coming from the depths of his green province, the idea of ration coupons remained a thoroughly abstract notion, and he complained bitterly to a headwaiter who was both vexed and long-suffering – and this really made Charles cross. Alice laughed, but he vowed to take her out that same evening to one of the very best black-market venues . . .

Outside on the pavement they looked at each other, smiling. The weather was fine the way it can be fine in Paris in summer.

'What are you doing this afternoon?' he asked.

'A bit of shopping,' she said in the same evasive voice. 'Shall we meet at the hotel in a little while?'

'Of course. Don't buy up all the stock,' he added teasingly.

For he knew before setting out that Alice's rendezvous with her conspirators was to take place on this first day in some nameless café. But where? According to the telephone call he had overheard that morning, it was to be the one where Jerome celebrated his last birthday with his henchmen – this was a very cryptic address. So cryptic that he was going to have to follow Alice like some detective from the Dubly agency that had fascinated him throughout his childhood. So at three o'clock they parted affectionately and Alice was a little shocked to see him set off so cheerfully for his business appointments when there was a chance he might never see her again. But Sambrat really was very frivolous; doubtless he was in love with her, but he was also very, very egotistic. She doubled back on herself a few times, went by the hotel again and came out via the rear entrance that Charles had pointed out to her. She finally ended up sitting on the terrace of the Café des Invalides, where she and Jerome and their friends had merrily got drunk on his thirtieth birthday. It was a quiet café, very sunny and very hot; and on this May afternoon a few tired Parisians, two provincials and a German soldier all seemed equally absorbed in the contemplation of their warm drinks. It was strange, thought Alice, how little nationality or civil status mattered in a heatwave. The few customers seemed to form a small provincial family that was overwhelmed by the heat, and that young man in his grey-green uniform sweating alongside them could almost be a distant relative.

She slowly sank into a mindless state in this café; the minutes passed, interminable minutes, and gradually doubt crept up on her, and with doubt came fear. It was twenty past four, Carnot was now fifteen minutes late, and that meant 'Get out' in every resistance network the world over. But Alice could not bring herself to leave. The thought of having come to Paris and all for nothing, of having stirred herself, committed herself, got worked up unnecessarily all of a sudden struck her with horror. She, who so desperately favoured darkness, anonymity, irresponsibility, suddenly couldn't stand them any more. She no longer wanted to live for nothing, fight for nothing, and die in vain, at the end of her long young life that she herself had already wrecked. Tears suddenly

[101]

sprang to her eyes and it was the fear of looking ridiculous and not fear of the Gestapo that she gave way to as she stood up.

Out in the street, she cut across towards the Military Academy; through her tears, the wide esplanade danced in the sun. She stumbled. A hand was laid on her arm, caught her and in that very instant she recognized Sambrat without even having time to fear anyone else's grip. It was Charles in his absurd light-coloured suit, with his absurd swell's face, and his absurd self-satisfied smile. It was Charles who, naturally, had followed her and scared off the real tail on her – the one who, under Jerome's instructions and in line with usual procedure, was on the look-out for anyone who might be following her. It was Charles who had sabotaged this first rendezvous and who was now going to make it necessary for her to go to a second rendezvous, and wait there, again, for twenty minutes, and then go to a third perhaps, if her contact didn't feel sufficiently reassured about approaching her. She hated him.

Charles was quite pleased with himself. Not only had he managed to follow Alice from a distance, not only had he witnessed her long wait from the café opposite – a wait that had shocked the gentleman in him and annoyed the lover – but what was more, he was here, now, to take her back, quite safely, away from these unpunctual and compromising characters. So the sudden pallor of Alice's face beneath her suntan and her cold eyes disconcerted him at first, before her words came through to him, words that she uttered in an alien voice (the kind of voice that in some films the rich bad guy adopts when speaking to the impoverished good guy, or the cruel industrialist to the faithful gardener); in any case, a voice that Alice would not have been thought capable of.

'What do you think you're doing?' she said. 'Are you mad?' And she went and sat on the nearest bench. He followed her, dumbfounded. She took a deep breath before continuing in a voice she obviously had difficulty in controlling, a voice venomous with scorn.

'How do you expect anyone to approach me if they can see you running along behind me wherever I go, as though I were a streetwalker? We're in the middle of a war, Charles, even if you won't accept it, despite the dark nights, people's wretchedness, the queues in the streets, despite all the hateful signs everywhere, there, and there, and there!'

And she pointed to the wooden noticeboards with German writing on them that were indeed all over Paris and that he had indeed so far failed to see. And what could he say to her? Nothing, except that he hadn't been able to see anything but her, and that if he were to take her to Cannes tomorrow he would no more be able to see the sea there than he had the Germans in Paris today.

'But I just wanted to protect you,' he said, 'to be sure that no one was following you, that . . .'

'Keep out of it, Charles. It's very kind of you to have come with me, but if you become a hindrance rather than a help I shall very easily manage without you.'

And she got up. She had regained some of her colour and her slim, elegant body stood out against the Paris sky and the dome of Les Invalides like some inaccessible object. The indulgent irony that then altered her voice didn't help matters.

'Go and see those POW employees of yours, or some old friend,' and she made it clear that she didn't even credit the friend he might meet with a female identity. 'And we'll go out this evening and eat in a very expensive restaurant where the steaks will be hidden under the salad and where we'll have a good laugh. But as for the

[103]

rest, it's nothing to do with you, as you've told me often enough.'

And with that she walked off without so much as a backward glance, certain, perfectly certain that he would not follow her any more; certain of his remorse, certain of his inevitable assent to her ventures into war. He went back to the hotel to savour alone the bitter fruits of devotion.

That evening, which he had hoped would be emotional if not amorous, turned out to be emotional indeed, but unhappy. His only recourse was to get drunk, which he attempted to do, in vain, on the atrocious, ruinously expensive cognac supplied by the concierge. He went to bed early and in desperate lucidity wrote three letters of apology to Alice: one impassioned, one sarcastic and one plaintive; then tore up all three and listened out for her.

Alice came back at about midnight and didn't go in to say goodnight to him. Charles waited half an hour in the dark until he couldn't hear the slightest sound in the room next door. He got up and went round to knock on her door from the corridor, feeling completely horrified to be doing so. Alice did not reply, no doubt pretending to be asleep, and afterwards he was grateful to her for this. Nevertheless, as he stood in the badly lit corridor, sweating and trembling outside the door of a woman he was importuning, Charles Sambrat realized with terror that on some other evening this same Sambrat might very well spend the night beating at some door, crying out a name, instead of very quickly going to bed without making a fuss, as he did tonight. And that other evening would see the birth of another Sambrat that he, Charles, had no regard for; a Sambrat who even disgusted him in advance.

Chapter Eight

THE WEATHER, like his mood, had deteriorated by the following morning. Charles woke up sad, was surprised at this, and took a few moments to remember why. 'Madame went out very early this morning, Monsieur Sambrat,' the concierge told him over the phone in a theatrical tone of voice in which Charles might perhaps have detected all the nuances had he been less obsessive. For the word 'madame', and 'madame' all by itself, not the concierge's usual 'Madame Sambrat', pointed to the concierge's admiration – even esteem – for Alice, whom he had instinctively recognized as a society lady, even though he had only very little experience of such women. As for his 'went out very early this morning', this contained doubt, alarm, indeed sarcasm. Whether out of excessive weariness or excessive enthusiasm, Monsieur Sambrat's conquests generally left his room after him. Finally, that solemn, pompous 'Monsieur Sambrat' actually implied some compassion, a farewell to victory, and just in case, a little sympathy, a few regrets for a past that was no longer. People respect unhappiness and find it especially hard to forgive success. The happiness of others is never bearable for very long, and all Charles's generosity could not prevent the concierge from being envious. Besides, not everything in the tone he adopted was misplaced: admiration was Alice's due, doubt and compassion were Charles's. (It is often so with the most injudicious comments on events, whether they're made by great historians or gossip columnists, concierges or society people; there's always a truthful aspect to them, though the truth itself is made up of nuances. Otherwise anyone could accuse Cole Porter of having plagiarized Beethoven's Fifth Symphony in 'Night and Day' – do, re, do, do, do, re, do, re – and be right; and, of course, wrong.)

The concierge's only mistake, his great mistake, was the elation in his voice that conjured up an image of a cheerful woman of easy virtue, dressed in short skirts, running round Paris in search of jewellery or furs. This was not the case. Alice had slept very badly. She had had nightmares and been afraid. And it was haste rather than jauntiness in her step when she set out in the direction of what was perhaps her destiny. Nevertheless she had followed Jerome's instructions to the letter. After that first rendezvous, made abortive by Charles's presence, she had telephoned her other contact in another cell; she had gone to the second rendezvous, where she had at last been joined by a partisan, a friend of Jerome, to whom she had explained the problem. It had been agreed that she would meet him again the very next day, very close to where they were to meet the others, so that if there was no trap, she could go fetch him and introduce him to the people waiting for them. Of course, with all those people gathered there after endless vicissitudes, after impossible journeys across a Europe in flames, with people whose nerves were shaken and who were often brokenhearted, it wasn't enough to be listened to: she had to be believed. Alice wondered whether she would get even that far; and then whether she would be able to persuade them to go somewhere else. Jerome's absence would already make this interim period more alarming, more suspect, for all those people who knew him, for whom Jerome was the contact, who had seen Alice when she'd been with him more as a friend of Jerome than an assistant.

When she got to the place where she was to meet them, she walked round the block three times, stopped at a chemist to buy some nail varnish, though she didn't really need any; but, stupidly, the mere act of buying such a frivolous thing at the last minute – something that would be completely useless as well (for who was going to worry whether her nails were well polished if she was tied to a post with a blindfold over her eyes?) – the mere fact of taking refuge in a frivolous past was reassuring. And it was with a resolute step that she headed towards number thirty-four and went through the gateway.

She came upon a long path with doors on either side of it, and at the far end, glistening in the Parisian sunshine, were some poppies and a few wild flowers that some poetic concierge had planted there. Alice walked slowly towards this pathetic garden, which struck her as fantastic, like the finest of paintings, the most brightly gleaming Douanier Rousseau, just as it seemed to her, in front of every door, that one of the men that she'd started to dream about at night, with knife-like faces and stony-pupilled eyes, was going to spring out. When she reached the garden she couldn't help crouching down and aimlessly picking a poppy – robbing the concierge, robbing the whole world, robbing death. And she knocked – three knocks, then two, then three – at the little wooden door to which the tenant's name – Monsieur Migond – was pinned with four drawing pins. After a moment's silence she knocked again, then a third time, knowing that this was the ritual, but nevertheless terrified that the door wouldn't be opened to her, and an old reflex, a very old pre-war reflex, made her knock more nervously. The door sprang open and she leapt back. This violent welcome was the work of a little white-haired, bespectacled man. He gave her a low bow and introduced himself as Monsieur Migond, tenant of the property; he smiled at her and waved her in with his left hand. She crossed the threshold and then saw those whom she'd come to save, or at least prevent from dying.

There were eight of them, no, ten, no, twelve: she couldn't keep count of them and her gaze went from one group to the other. There were twelve silent individuals, individuals who were almost sexless, ageless and faceless, so much had fear, the will to live, anxiety and horror eaten away at them. Their faces were at the same time the most awful and the most handsome faces Alice had ever seen. For a moment she almost knelt down and humbly begged their pardon on behalf of every one of her Aryan – supposedly Aryan – brothers; of everyone in France, Germany or elsewhere who believed them to be different from themselves. It was fortunate that some instinctive shyness and pride prevented her from doing so, for they were staring at her, or looking up at her with eyes full of deference and absolute trust.

'Do you recognize me?' she said. 'I'm Jerome's wife.'

She heard herself say 'wife' and was surprised by this bourgeois instinct of hers, realized at once that it was the only way of giving them a little reassurance. And that, even at a time like this, when everything was failing, self-destructing, when all social and human laws, all societies, taboos and criteria – all mere houses of cards – were flying apart, and the words 'decency' and 'virtue' were completely outmoded and of as much use to a woman as a daisy on his helmet is to a soldier, she realized that it was all the same more reassuring for these people to think of her as Jerome's wife than as his mistress.

'I didn't know that Jerome had already got married.

[108]

I'm so happy for him! That was his dream, you know? He spoke to me so often about it, spoke of you, Alice, so often, to myself and Jean-Pierre.' This was a pretty young woman talking, who was gesturing towards her husband, a tall thin man – Alice remembered Jerome telling her he was the best architect in Paris.

'But where is Monsieur Jerome?' said a fat lady, suddenly stepping forward, holding two toddlers by the hand as though they were both proof of her importance. Judging by the state of their faces, both had colds. 'He promised to save my children! He must save them! I don't mind if I die!' she concluded, slumping onto a chair and sobbing, to the great shame, it seemed, of her companions, her children and the master of the house.

'Now then,' said Alice in a condescending, authoritative tone of voice, one that sounded superior and far removed from her actual state of mind, 'now then, madame, we promised to do something and we're here to do it. Jerome is involved in a very big operation and I've been given the job of looking after you. Our orders have been changed so as to make sure nothing happens to you. There's a different person to help get you out – I'm going to fetch him and introduce him to you in a couple of minutes, if that's all right with you. There. Is everything OK now? Is everyone happy about that?'

She was smiling; she was smiling especially at the young woman to whom Jerome had so often spoken about their possible marriage. That Jerome, so secretive and yet so trusting and above all so full of hope! She couldn't imagine herself married to Jerome, nor anyone else for that matter. It was strange. What was she doing here? How did this crazy situation come about? What was she doing here, near this little garden with its poppies, with this woman talking to her about Jerome as though he were her husband, with these women and children whom strangers wanted to kill? What kind of madness was this? Everything was spinning round in her head, it was all so crazy, her knees were giving way. The young woman must have noticed, for she quickly pulled up a chair for her and laid both hands on her shoulders.

'You must be shattered,' she said. 'I'm Lydia Strauss. Jerome must have spoken to you about us.'

'Of course, of course,' said Alice, lying insistently and closing her eyes.

'You must be dead tired and here we are staring at you without even offering you something to drink!' exclaimed Monsieur Migond in distress. He scurried over to a sideboard from which he drew out a bottle of claret, an old Bordeaux that was much older than he was, judging by the dust it was covered with.

'We'll all drink a toast.'

'That's a very good idea,' said Alice. 'Let's drink a toast. You know, the hardest part is over now. Everything's going to be marvellously well organized . . . The main thing is that we should have met here today,' she concluded before leaning forward a little. She had even rested her head on the table in a display of complete abandon; she had been over-frightened, she realized. She felt her whole body turn to liquid, felt her hair come away from her scalp, her skin being completely torn away from her body by invisible hands; gradually she felt she was going to faint there and then.

'My God,' said Lydia, 'Jean-Pierre, help me . . .'

They lifted her head and bathed her brow with water. The fat woman patted her hands and the snotty-nosed children stared at her sympathetically. No, they weren't more especially handsome than other people, they weren't more especially crafty, they weren't more especially wicked, they weren't more especially anything; they were like her, people like her, except that they were perhaps less absurd, and obviously less fortunate than

[110]

she was. She smiled, for no particular reason. Gradually, and to her great surprise, they all began to laugh, softly at first, then a little louder, then perhaps even a little too loudly, since the kindly Monsieur Migond, abandoning his bottle and glasses, rushed to the centre of the room, stood on tiptoe and raised his arms above his head – arms that signalled for quiet, like some conductor begging his musicians to stop playing at once.

The weather remained unsettled all day long; showers and sunshine followed one another so quickly, patches of shadow and light were so rapidly interspersed on the pavements that the whole of Paris seemed to be in the shadow of a zebra. Where had he read that? Love was turning him into a very sorry seducer and a very poor poet.

Charles was officially in Paris to get one of his engineers, a POW in Germany, repatriated. He trailed round from office to office, looking grumpy and irascible, which meant that his applications met with a great deal more success than usual and the realization that this was so exasperated him. If you now had to shout and yell like these Teutons and click your heels like them in order to work in industry, then Jerome was right; these bawling braggarts had to be driven out of this gentle land of France. Besides, whatever he might have said three days ago, he found the presence of these soldiers, these orderlies, these guards scattered about everywhere, in the streets, in sentry boxes, in ministerial corridors, less and less tolerable. You didn't get used to it, you came up against it ever more frequently, jarring your eyes, your nerves, and your pride as well. The Germans' natural arrogance was less humiliating than their affected courtesy. In any case there was something about them – it might have been their underlying nature, or purely and simply their uniform – that made him sweat horribly (and he was a man with a dry skin), and come out of their offices feeling exhausted. A simple matter of repatriation, of someone's anticipated liberation, was no justification for him to be in this physical state. He went back to the hotel, feeling angry and exasperated. If he got any more worked up, he too would end up by taking to the maquis in the Dauphiné with his shotgun, and joining tearaways younger than himself. Now that would go down well in the factory, both with the workers and the shareholders!

It was six o'clock and Alice was late, of course, Charles grumbled, forgetting that if Alice had arranged to meet anyone at all it was the concierge, and this allowed her a certain delay. At six-thirty, and then at quarter to seven Charles's reproachfulness gave way to anxiety. She must have got involved in some madness; and in spite of her 'friends' she was perhaps in prison right now, in the hands of some army rabble; and recalling the face of one frosty orderly, Charles was gripped by a kind of cold nausea that made him sit down on his bed, trembling like a young girl. 'But where is she?' he said to himself. 'But what's happening to me?' was his next thought. 'But where is she? What's happening to me?' And these two questions were almost equally cruel. He was lighting a cigarette with shaking hands when the door of the adjacent room opened, closed again, and there was the sound of Alice's footsteps striking the floor. Inhaling deeply, Charles fell back onto the still-fresh pillowcase, closed his eyes and dropped his match on the bedside rug. He couldn't remember having experienced such fear in his whole life, nor such relief, though this might be premature, for he had an answer to only one of his questions; though he now knew where Alice was, he still didn't know what was happening to him.

And now he was smoking in silence, indifferent to Alice's nearby presence, to her plans, her destiny – to

[112]

their destiny. He felt good, as weary and serene as an old man, though his only desire was to regress, to be with his mother again, in the meadow behind the house, and to be ten years old. His life since then had been nothing but an extended farce from every point of view. And he felt vaguely put out when he heard a knock at his door. He got up, opened the door, and met again with Alice's face and Alice's gaze, and rediscovered the charms of being a man and an adult, as well as a terrible feeling of impotence, of rebellion, at seeing Alice come into his room and, as always happened, thereby destroy the thousand Alices conjured up in her absence by his memory, his imagination and his desire, the thousand Alices he'd made accessible to himself. All his plaster Alices became colourless and boring once he had the beautiful, distinct, precious, graspable, unpredictable Alice here in front of him. 'Ah! One day I shall have this Alice too!' was the thought that suddenly came to him in a rush of impatience and vulgarity – a vulgarity extremely rare in him, a man so little given to that jovial scorn of women that he so much hated in other men. But he didn't even reproach himself for it, he was already far away; he was running away, he didn't know where, but at top speed.

'Are you all right, Charles?'

Alice's voice was a little perturbed, anxious. And he smiled at her. Yet he felt an odd contraction contort the lower half of his face into an almost painful crease very close to the ugly grimace that is the same in adults, babes-in-arms or old folk, and is a prelude to tears.

He had automatically risen from his bed when she came in, but he sat down on it again after having gestured to her to sit down in the mock Regency armchair by the fireplace. He had both feet on the wooden floor and his hands on his knees. He looked like a contrite schoolboy

[113]

who'd been punished. Alice, who had at last had a successful day, suddenly felt the soul of indulgence. She smiled at him.

'Did you have a good day, Charles? Did you find out anything about that first-rate engineer of yours?'

'Yes, I think it will turn out all right,' he said in such a serious, confidential tone of voice that neither of them could skate over the ludicrousness of the intonation and just looked at each other in embarrassment, Alice on the verge of laughter and Charles ready to fall into confusion.

'Well,' she said, 'what's happening?'

'Nothing,' he said, standing up and stretching unconsciously, as though he were on his own; and still as though he were on his own, he added: 'Nothing, except that I've realized that I could be very unhappy on your account. And that it didn't matter . . . well, that it wouldn't stop me.'

'What do you mean, it doesn't matter?' said Alice laughing, being thoroughly flirtatious. 'What do you mean? When you're so obviously meant to be happy! I should hate to see you unhappy.'

'Prove it,' said Charles without any insolence, and even with some gentleness.

And he opened the door of his room and stood aside to let her pass. The light, which was on a time-switch, went out before they had reached the landing where the lift was. Having turned round in the semi-darkness towards Charles, Alice was surprised, almost frightened, to find him so close to her, and took a step backwards. His only reaction to this defensive gesture was a slightly sad smile, the smile of a silenced man, a smile that finally worried Alice. She didn't want a Charles who was unhappy or a loser; it frightened her. It made her sad, and disappointed her. She had very quickly, too quickly perhaps, grown accustomed to defending herself against

[114]

his charm, against his desire for her. Once disarmed, this adversary disconcerted her. Dear God, she was behaving just like a whore! After all, shouldn't she be delighted to see him being reasonable? And she realized that she had never wanted him to be indifferent, that his indifference would be supremely disagreeable to her. This petit-bourgeois individual, so eager and so natural, so disarming and so ingenuous in his grown-up cynicism, so concerned for his comfort and his games – this petit-bourgeois represented adventure to her (in a limited field, one which she'd yet to play on, the field of physical pleasure) – yes, he represented adventure . . .

The dark corridors of this pseudo-luxurious hotel with its lewd concierge, its rooms with over-large beds, and its romantic eighteenth-century engravings that came straight off a production line, Charles's convertible, the gaudy rocking chairs on the terrace at Formoy – this whole decor disturbed her. It evoked a bawdy and spuriously poetic bourgeoisie, and it disturbed her more than other decors she'd come across before, decors more refined and more natural, whose refinement was of the kind that only a great deal of money can extract from luxury, and whose naturalness only a great deal of money can extract from what's natural. The kind of refinement that brings palatial corridors wide enough to allow people to walk past each other, and an unseen discreet staff, carpets deeper than the mattresses, as well as completely empty meadows, private limousines carrying anonymous passengers, and virgin beaches; in fact, if it already took a large fortune to capture the public's interest, it took an enormous one to drop from public memory. She was not from the same background as Charles, and this was the first time this thought had occurred to her; and what's more, now was just the time, in the midst of war and privation, to take account of it.

She had never considered this in relation to Jerome, but that was because Jerome had no liking for outward signs either of his own background or other people's. If she had for one moment been concerned about such things, it would have occurred to her that she could take Jerome anywhere, but perhaps not Charles . . . And yet she loved Charles's lock of hair in the breeze, she loved his pride in his car, his delight in treating her to this hotel, even his vanity in wearing his dreadful fitted jacket. What did it matter whether what he liked was in good or bad taste, as long as he had a strong liking for it . . . And now he was ready not to love or suffer any more because of her. It was an aberration of destiny . . . unless it was the cunning wile of a seducer. In any case, she didn't put up much of a protest when, after some impenetrable discussion with his dreadful accomplice at the reception desk, he announced that they were going to dine to the playing of violins. She even agreed to go and dig out from the bottom of her travelling case (that had been repacked in the meantime) a very décolletée evening dress – Charles liked them décolletée – and to change into it. Meanwhile, Charles forgot his sad destiny, sentimentally speaking, and feeling wild with joy, got himself into a dinner jacket made to measure by the best tailor in Valence.

Chapter Nine

ACCORDING TO the hotel concierge and the Paris gossip columns, the *Aiglon* in the rue de Berri was the nightclub then in vogue. A well-conducted orchestra played a variety of tempos, and a marvellous violinist who wouldn't admit to being anything but Hungarian – though despite his stubborn denials you could tell he was a gypsy – brought tears to everyone's eyes. Current celebrities, the stars of stage and screen, literary and journalistic personalities regularly put in an appearance there, as though to put an *Ausweis* stamp on their stardom. The most classy German officers took their French female conquests there, and with the music to help relax everyday practices, everyone who was anybody in Paris had some marvellous evenings in this place. To get a table so late in the day had cost a small fortune, but Charles, who was spendthrift by nature as it was, would have given the shirt off his back to dance with Alice, to hold her in his arms for two minutes, to feel Alice standing against him, to guide her steps in time with his own rhythm and only incidentally in time with the rhythm the orchestra was playing. This is what he dreamed of doing.

He dreamed of it, but ever since he had seen Alice come down from her room again with her body sheathed in a tight-fitting evening dress the same blue-grey colour as her eyes, from which emerged a single bare shoulder and a single bare arm, his dream had become more clearly defined, indeed far too clearly defined; he was prey to a desire that was animal, brutal, almost painful, that left him stunned, and that Alice's every word, her every gesture and every glance seemed to intensify. It was a man struck dumb who entered the nightclub and made his way between the tables, following Alice after the headwaiter. The voices, the laughter, the music, the crystal, the German uniforms, the dinner jackets, the women – these were no more than a pointless, noisy background, an abstract background arranged anyhow around the only real and tangible thing about this evening: Alice walking ahead of him, then Alice seated in front of him; Alice whom he would perhaps have to rape one of these days, if she didn't succumb to him very soon. He opened the menu with trembling hands, and his face looked so haggard, so pale that once again she grew worried.

'Are you feeling unwell, Charles?'

But as he stammered out some paltry excuses, she again forgot about it, battling herself against feelings of malaise that were less physical but just as violent as his. She was beginning to hate this place, to be frightened by it. The table next to theirs, the table just behind Charles, was occupied by two German officers – circumstances had made bachelors of them and they were very quiet compared with their compatriots. They were speaking a fairly cultivated German, she realized, and when she raised her head slightly she saw that they were both rather handsome, that the look in their eyes expressed neither arrogance nor scorn, and that if they seemed bored they were nevertheless being polite about it. Charles, on the other hand, had been stubbornly avoiding meeting her gaze for nearly an hour now, ever since they had changed, if the truth be told.

'Do you dislike my dress as much as all that?' she said smiling, but half-serious all the same, so long ago was it since she had felt at all desirable. And as Charles's face was taking on a look of indignation at this supposition, she very quickly added: 'You haven't spoken to me since I put on this dress, does that mean you don't like it?'

'I like it only too much,' said Charles with some abruptness. 'Listen, Alice, I've behaved like a fool, I know, I'm not used to women – at least, not to women like you. Nor to being in love,' he added, attempting to laugh and raising a glass of white wine to his lips – his fifth glass in ten minutes and one that would probably be no more efficacious than the first four.

'But you must have been in love before now,' said Alice, she too smiling, with some effort right now, as the German officer's gaze came and rested on her.

'Oh yes, of course,' replied Charles, 'at least I think so, but it didn't frighten me.'

'Because you were certain of achieving your goal?' she asked. There was a sad irony in her voice that all of a sudden distressed Charles. She really took him for some little cock-of-the-walk.

'No, of course not,' he said drily, 'I wasn't sure of being loved in return. Who can be? But I was sure of being able to run away very quickly.'

'And in this case it's me who would run away, is that it?' said Alice, using a conditional tense that he understood to refer to the very near future – she could see it in his eyes, and against her better judgement she placed her hand on his.

'I would leave, even if I loved you, Charles, I would have to leave, you know I would.'

'Oh no,' said Charles. 'If you loved me too, you

[119]

wouldn't leave. I can't believe that any woman could prefer an idea to a man! The opposite, yes, because men are stupid, but not women!'

'You're wrong there,' she said, but only half-heartedly because the officer at the next table had got up and was heading towards their table. He stopped in front of them and bowed deeply.

'Might I request the pleasure of this dance?' he said in French, with a slight accent and in a perfectly courteous tone of voice.

Charles looked at him in amazement. It was true, the orchestra was playing and people were dancing and he hadn't even noticed; he in turn got to his feet.

'Madame is with me,' he said shortly.

The officer turned towards him and looked hard at him. He was a good-looking man, blond, with a sad but nonetheless arrogant air about him, and Charles was overcome with a desire for a fight, a desire that momentarily restored the use of his five senses to him. There was a silence, during which Alice paled to the point of fainting.

'If Madame is with you,' said the officer, repeating the words, 'that's fine. I wanted to see if you deserved her. Your compatriots sometimes lend us their lady companions. My deepest apologies, madame,' he said, bowing towards Alice, and he turned away.

Charles sat down again, surprised and vaguely disappointed. He cast a glance at Alice, who was regaining her colour, and who returned his gaze with a smile.

'He's absolutely right,' said Charles. 'Let's dance. I hadn't even asked you to.'

Ever since he was old enough to leap about on dance floors, Charles Sambrat had been regarded, if not as a superb dancer, then at least as an agreeable partner. His enthusiasm was unbounded, so too was his vigour, if not his gracefulness and technique. He avoided collisions, his steps were not complicated, he very evidently danced with the comfort and pleasure of his partner in mind, and not the admiration of the crowd. But Alice was in grave danger of remaining ignorant of this reputation and, even more so, of not subscribing to it. He stumbled as he took hold of her and then persisted in keeping her at a distance, at arm's length, looking stiff and miserable all the while. He breathed through his mouth, with difficulty, and tirelessly cut across the dance floor like some old labourer digging furrows, from left to right, from the centre to the edge, with greater or lesser speed, depending on the orchestra's tempo. Alice had actually attempted a supposedly Argentinian figure in the course of the first tango, she had even leant backwards slightly on Charles's arm, supple in her movement; but, first in amazement and then in panic, she had seen him bend over her, fascinated, and simultaneously incline himself in her direction, and she had only managed to prevent their both falling over by miraculously heaving herself up. Since then, she had given up and, cutting diagonally across the floor, had docilely covered the same distance as her partner.

They must have done about five or six kilometres in this fashion, she estimated, flashing little smiles of apology at the couples cut up by Charles, who evidently wouldn't stand for the least obstacle in his path. When eventually this forced march seriously got on her nerves, Alice looked up at Charles: he, meanwhile, was whistling the tune of 'Pink cherry trees, white apple trees' while the orchestra's tremulous violins attacked, for perhaps the tenth time, 'I'm alone tonight'. To attract the attention of this frenzied deaf-mute, she clutched at his sleeves and crossed her flat-heeled shoes on the dance floor; Charles stared at her in bewilderment, and slowly came to a halt, stopping in mid tune, right there in the middle of the dance floor (where several couples who had already been jostled by him – and were evidently hostile – directed ugly glances at them).

'What were you saying?' asked Charles, 'I didn't hear you.'

'I said – ' (Alice was shouting to make herself heard over the unbridled playing of the orchestra) ' – that if we were to become separated by one of your arabesques we would meet up at our table, all right? What do you say?'

He nodded his head gravely. He didn't hear what Alice was saying. For nearly half an hour now, he had been trying to hide from her the absurd and untimely excitement of his intractable body, to disguise from this refined woman his state of schoolboyish frustration. He felt obscene and ridiculous. There was no question but that this evening, like the rest of their stay here, would be a catastrophe.

He had until then been studiously gazing at the walls of the nightclub. He couldn't bring himself to look down on this calm, trustful, upturned face. Like some startled horse, he gave her a quick glance; then, with an inane and enthusiastic smile, returned his gaze to the orchestra.

'I don't understand,' he stammered, 'don't you like my arabesques? Perhaps they're old-fashioned?'

Alice's burst of laughter clearly astonished him. She had literally exploded, and now, with her whole body jerking and her head resting on his chest, she was hiccoughing.

'I was joking, I was joking. Arabesques? Good God, Charles, I was joking! What arabesques? . . . We've been travelling east to west, north to south for the past quarter of an hour! I swear to you my remark was purely ironic. But what arabesques, for God's sake?'

She was laughing so much and so heartily that all of

[122]

a sudden Charles relaxed too, seized with another fit of laughter that was both nervous and relieved, and without conferring, they returned to their table and sank into their chairs. Neither really knew what the other was laughing about, but they laughed at themselves, and they laughed over these two wasted days that had been hateful for both of them. They laughed at finding themselves together again, and Charles laughed especially at having recovered himself, the happy Sambrat. In fact, he resented the terrified Sambrat that he'd been, the Sambrat who'd felt humiliated for no reason, as he would have resented a total stranger. And added to his resentment was a kind of terror. For all his present lucidity, he wouldn't be able to prevent his absurd, scared double from returning, from looming up again and usurping his place – whenever, wherever, howsoever that might happen.

Meanwhile, on the other side of the table, Alice was laughing like a child. A desirable child, of course, but a child all the same, and like a child, she had to be kept amused. And oddly, having at last forgotten about his virility, Charles felt like a man again. He drank, he danced, he sang, he made fleeting contact with Alice's shoulder, her cheek, her hair. In short he flirted, with all the techniques and enthusiasm imaginable, his past and present conspiring to advise him. And at the same time Alice enjoyed herself. She was a tiny bit drunk, and she leaned on him while they were dancing, her pupils dilated and her mouth slightly swollen with alcohol. Alice would soon be his, either this evening or some other evening, if he didn't revert to his passion-inspired fantasies, if he didn't forget that she was a woman like other women and that, what's more, she hadn't found him all that unattractive during the past forty-eight hours.

To finish with, the orchestra struck up with a few of

[123]

those old 1930s tunes; the tunes of their adolescence and first loves, tunes of nearly ten years ago, tunes that made them feel slightly nostalgic – with the imprecise, nameless, nostalgia that is the only nostalgia to allow the present to pass happily, that makes one regretful, not so much that the past should be so far distant, but that the present should have been so long in coming. The kind of nostalgia that makes you think you can see your youth dancing away somewhere, happy and sad at the same time, lonely and deprived of the partner now with you, who made the mistake of not sharing your youth. A sentimental, unfair kind of nostalgia, a nostalgia so self-centred that it makes you ask your current companion, without the least cynicism, the question that, for all its banality, is the height of dishonesty: 'Why weren't you there?' A question in which one reproaches one's new lover for the pleasures and happiness one enjoyed in the past with someone else; as though, in other words, it was a matter of some shortcoming on our lover's part and not rather some error of our own; as though, in our retrospective jealousy, only our lover's tardiness can be blamed and not our own impatience. The cynicism and dishonesty are completely unconscious and completely natural. No one remembers having been hungry or having hunted for something once one has found it and been satiated. One's recollection of oneself is of an inattentive solitary prey that has been tracked down and caught, more or less willingly, by someone else. One never recalls having been the hunter as well, one forgets that there's often a moment when the roles of hunted and hunter are reversed and that, generally speaking, this leads to the greater pleasure of both.

Chapter Ten

BECAUSE OF the curfew, the nightclub closed at a quarter to midnight, and as the hotel wasn't far, Alice and Charles decided to walk back. The night was light blue around them, dark blue further in the distance, and along the Champs-Elysées all the buildings were dark grey and looked as though surprised to see these two joyful and solitary pedestrians pass by. The avenues were deserted, there was a smell of the countryside around them, for there had been showers and squalls over Paris while they were dancing and the town they were now walking through was fresh, new and gleaming. Indeed, the wind must have been tremendous for the chestnut trees had lost their young leaves to it, and these were now scattered about, stuck to the pavements, turning towards the sky an indignant tender green.

Alice had taken Charles's arm very naturally, and they were walking in step, like some old couple, across this empty town. Paris belonged to them; the Champs-Elysées descended very gently towards their hotel. They slipped through town, their feet tired from too much dancing, their voices from too much laughter and their ears from too much music, not forgetting their eyes and lips that were tired from too much smoke and bad cognac. They laughingly recalled the arrogance of certain members of the occupying forces, the obsequiousness of certain maîtres d'hôtel, the excitement and embarrassment of certain women and the perfect naturalness and casualness of others. Setting aside the officer's preposterous invitation, Charles found the Germans relatively correct, whereas Alice actually saw correctness in none bar that officer. But she refused to discuss the matter. She couldn't remember having had so much fun and feeling so young and cheerful for years. Of course, she owed this to alcohol and to Charles's newfound good humour; but neither alcohol nor Charles would have had the same success even a year ago. She was getting better, better by the minute, she would pull through! Or maybe it was her clear conscience, the risk she had taken in going to that sinister place, that moment of terror at that closed door, her first engagement, her first effort, the first effort she was at last making for someone other than herself, for something other than the anguished encroaching muddle that her own spirit had turned into – for centuries already, for centuries.

How horrible! How could she have put up with herself for so long? How could anyone else have put up with her? How could Jerome have loved her, taken masochism so far as to love her? And she hated herself for giving the name masochism or eccentricity to that immense tenderness, that infinite patience that she knew was a wonderful love; just as she had vaguely despised herself a little while ago for having danced the charleston with such high spirits when she knew that Tolpin, Faroux and Dax were dead. These were Jerome's three best aides, but for her they were just half-glimpsed faces, shadows, of the grey-and-white faced men who had become Jerome's only friends. But she mustn't confuse her little fits of euphoria and depression with the destiny of her country and its liberty, which is what she was in the process of doing, in spite of herself. Once a plaintive Alice, she was going to turn into an absurd Alice. Oh! if only she could stop thinking about herself for a moment, it was always herself! If only she could stop this whining navel-gazing! If only . . . She made an effort to listen to Charles. What was he saying?

'If by some miracle we survive,' he was saying beside her, 'I shall take you drinking and dancing there, but it'll be real champagne. However, I'd be surprised if we make it . . .'

'But why you?' said Alice, suddenly shocked, even horrified, by Charles's funereal tone of conviction. How could this optimist who hadn't got mixed up in the war foresee such short destinies for them?

'Why?' he said. 'Because I'm just a man, just a human being – as you know,' he said laughing, 'and I can't see anything but a camel being able to withstand all that.'

She glanced at him in astonishment, which seemed to astonish him too.

'But what are you talking about?' she asked in a quavering, terrified voice, the voice of an old woman; a senile voice that all of a sudden was desperately clinging to life.

'But I'm talking to you about that vile liquid they served us under the name of cognac,' said Charles. 'Can you believe it, we drank nearly the whole bottle between us?'

And Alice's relief must have been quite obvious, since he took her by the arm and led her along without another word, apart from an 'I see!' delivered in a sympathetic tone of voice, with scarcely a trace of amusement in it, that almost drove Alice into his arms with tears in her eyes. That almost made her say to Charles, like a heroine in some serial, 'I was so frightened. And I am frightened, very frightened.' And Alice was ingenuously surprised to discover in herself, afterwards, the possibility that she might enjoy life: the possibility that losing her life might be repellent to her.

It was where the rue Royale comes into the Place Concorde that the incident took place. Within a moment the silence and darkness of the town became so many traps. As though on the huge set of some director who'd turned into a raving madman, spotlights illuminated anonymous extras; lorries with locked brakes came screaming past within a hair's breadth of the obelisk; gunshots that would have been incongruous at any time whistled out towards the Seine and transformed the peaceful, pastoral city – for the past two years it had been returned to carriages and pedestrians, to the slow pace of 1900 – transformed it into a modern capital at war and in danger. Charles was holding Alice by the wrist. He watched open-mouthed as a lorry with blinding headlights came towards them. He only just reacted in time to place himself at the last moment between Alice and the headlights. Two soldiers in grey-green uniform, looking mulish and vacant, climbed down with their guns trained on Charles and Alice. Violent blasts on a whistle, coming from behind them now, made them turn round. Another patrol was arriving, 'yelling like cretins as well,' thought Charles, with their guns trained not on them this time but on some ageless, colourless shadow – only afterwards did they notice the bleeding face and the hands tied behind the person's back. This stranger was reeling from one soldier to another, and each of them shoved him away again violently, to the accompaniment of laughter and a kind of satisfied snarling, like that of dogs on a fox hunt. A more brutal shove made him stumble and fall at the feet of two motionless officers, and this stilled the pack, bringing it to attention. Alice had lowered her eyes. She was pale. She was squeezing Charles's hand in her own. She

[128]

seemed to be listening to something coming from far away, something much more frightening than what was happening in front of her; in any event, something that she'd been acquainted with for a long time already.

'Papers, *schnell*,' said the officer. 'You had a rendezvous with this man here, *nein?* You're terrorists? Get in, *schnell, schnell.*'

'But no, no, we've been dancing,' said Charles, feeling aggravated, 'we've just left the *Aiglon*. Telephone them, they'll tell you. We're going back to our hotel, rue de Rivoli. Here are my papers.'

'Get in, *schnell, schnell,* get in, *schnell,*' the fair-haired one yelled, suddenly turning nasty. He had just become aware of Alice – until then she'd been concealed by Charles and by the darkness – and the sight of this young woman, of her beauty and apparent indifference, seemed to infuriate him. And as Charles dithered, consulting Alice with a glance – as if there was any choice to make – the officer motioned his henchmen towards them with a jerk of his chin. They seized Charles by the elbow and when he struggled they threw him to the ground at Alice's feet, alongside the stranger, the famous terrorist – which was what he'd actually become in Charles's eyes, for this stranger had destroyed everything, everything, including the amused congeniality, the almost confessed attraction Alice felt towards Charles – and the even more fragile hope he had entertained of spending the night with her, in their lovely white hotel-bed, with their windows open on the chestnut trees in the Tuileries, and on the dawn that would break to the left, over the Tolbiac bridge; the dawn following their first sleepless night together; the dawn that they would watch together, leaning over the balcony, shivering, tired and relaxed, promising each other a thousand similar dawns. That's what this poor boy had unwittingly wrecked, the boy and these swastika-ed bullies.

[129]

The lorry smelt of petrol, damp rags and vomit. In fact it stank of fear, a smell that Charles instantly recognized as the smell on the farm where he and his detachment had taken refuge after having stupidly challenged that tank; the smell on the farm where Lechat had died. But it was a short journey.

The barracks in the Place Saint-Augustin was a hideous but imposing-looking building where, even at this late hour, you saw nothing but clean-shaven jaws in the corridors, and heard nothing but well-polished boots clicking against one another. They went down corridor after corridor, through halls, up and down staircases, always surrounded by the baying men, bristling strangely with arms, who ended up by quick-marching them into a white room where a desk stood waiting beneath a portrait of Hitler. A soldier pointed them to some chairs. They sat on the edge of them while the terrorist was thrown to the ground, then dragged by the feet to another room. They saw him as he went past – disfigured with blows, his clothes in tatters, hugging his chest in his arms, in pain. Charles offered him a cigarette as he passed, and the man tried to take it with an attempt at a smile, a smile his jaw made obviously impossible.

'Are you in pain?' asked Alice. The orderly yelled in German and she shrugged her shoulders. Anyway, the officer was now returning, accompanied by a junior officer – a captain – who looked older, calmer and more disquieting. He stared the two men in the face, as though they were livestock, but gave Alice an ironic, old-world kiss of the hand.

'So,' he said, sitting behind the desk, 'you've been disguising yourself as a man of the world, a reveller, a socialite, in order to meet your terrorist friends?'

This speech was addressed to Charles. 'That's what it means, doesn't it, the Champs-Elysées at night? Your papers are excellent, my compliments. You also make cardboard shoes, I believe?' he asked abruptly.

'Since your arrival, yes indeed,' said Charles, who was gradually developing a hatred of this fellow, and was fed up with remaining calm, despite Alice's silent prayers. In any case, their night was ruined now, he might as well have a little fun at the expense of these louts.

'Are you married, madame?'

'Yes.'

'Yes, *mein capitaine*,' said the man in a gentle voice. For he was very gentle, too gentle – his voice, his gestures and the look in his eye were too gentle.

'Not to this gentleman? Nor the one who's gone?' he said, pointing to Charles and the trail of blood left on the ground by the terrorist.

'No.'

'No, *mein capitaine*. But that's no obstacle, is it?' said the man, lighting a cigarette. 'You go out with this gentleman and your husband's happy all the same? Or doesn't he know?'

'I'm divorced,' said Alice coldly, 'and my husband is living in the USA . . . *mein capitaine*.'

'Why did you marry an American when there are so many Europeans prepared to adore you here, aren't there? Don't you agree, Monsieur . . . Monsieur Sambrat,' he said, flicking open Charles's identity card. Charles was drawing shallow breaths to calm himself. 'Speaking for myself,' said the officer, 'I'd be very happy to . . . anyone here would be happy to marry you, eh? So why did you marry an American?'

But what does this pig-headed drunkard with his convoluted sentences want with me? thought Alice, who suddenly felt that her strength and emotions were exhausted. She was no longer thinking of the organization nor of the very little she knew about it, nor of the necessity that she remain to all intents and purposes the

[131]

Alice Fayatt whom a few Parisian salons and a few influential snobs would vouch for (people beyond all suspicion of rebellion and courage, but whose concern for frivolity, and therefore, in that world, for order, was guaranteed). She was exhausted and the idea that she might at that very moment have been lying beside Charles in the absurdly ornate, large bed in the hotel passed through her mind as something quite ridiculous. She glanced at him and saw he was tense, strained, that he had a dark look in his eye, and she found him handsome.

'My husband was not American, he was Austrian,' she said in a weary voice.

'So this Austrian leaves a pretty woman like you all alone in Vienna, with its waltzes? Was that the reason for the divorce?'

He was laughing, but mirthlessly, and his teasing seemed as tedious to utter as it was to listen to. It was almost out of charity that Alice replied, 'My husband was Austrian, but he was also Jewish. Do you see, *mein capitaine?*'

There was a slightly longer pause than before. The captain gradually seemed to get his breath back.

'Aryan certificate,' he said in a dry bureaucratic voice, no longer a joking voice. Her face suddenly relaxed, Alice opened her handbag and drew out a long stamped document and handed it to the soldier standing beside her.

The officer read it carefully without once raising his eyes to look at Alice, and it was also with his back turned to her that he said, as he put the paper down on his desk, 'I hope that you now prefer Aryans? Or do you miss that small scar, that small difference in Jewish men? No? Is that why you liked them? Or was it their money you liked? The contents of trouser pockets are all the same to women, aren't they? *Achtung!*' he shouted as

[132]

Charles leapt from his chair, over the desk and seized him by the throat.

It was a good fight in which Charles came off worse, naturally, but only after a few moments. Alice had hidden her face in her hands at the sight of Charles taking the first punch and removed them when the men's panting and the hammering of fists on an inert body had ceased. Charles was propped sideways in his chair, with his head hanging backwards and his hair in a mess. He was breathing noisily, groaning a little, and a stream of blood ran down his temples, making his hair – normally so shiny, so clean, so smooth – all sticky; and oddly, this trivial injury to his attractiveness made Alice more indignant than his grimace of pain, or his groaning. In a while, back at the hotel, I'll wash his head, she thought stubbornly, the concierge is sure to give me some hot water as the water from the tap is too lukewarm. And I'll give him a real shampoo.

The two soldiers, whose hair was also messed by the fight, and one of whom was already sporting a blue-black eye, were holding Charles by the shoulders. They tightened their grip when he opened his eyes. Charles saw Alice as he came to, and automatically smiled at her before noticing the captain behind his desk, where-upon he scowled like a schoolboy. There was something comical and unreal about this scene, thought Alice.

'So,' said the captain, coming towards Charles, 'you don't like jokes? You're Jewish too, perhaps? We'll soon see.'

And he gestured towards a third soldier, who started laughing, went over to Charles, and in spite of his kicks and insults, set about pulling down his trousers. Alice looked away. Charles's cries of rage made her feel sick and drove her to despair.

'Look, madame, and now compare him with your husband,' said the captain, and as she did not stir, he added, 'Or if you prefer, he can stay like this until tomorrow morning.'

Then she turned towards Charles. He was standing there half-naked, with this trousers heaped around his ankes, his shirt and dinner jacket held back by the soldiers. She saw his lowered eyelids and his humiliated face filled with shame. Then she called him by name, her voice charged with all the seductiveness she was capable of. When she had met his evasive eyes, she deliberately lowered her own to the lower half of his body and raised them only very slowly. And it was with a little nod of approval, a look full of the most undisguised respect that she gave Charles a radiant, delighted smile of unbounded promise of the most precious kind – a smile that left Charles as red-faced and dumbfounded as his gaolers.

It wasn't until dawn that they left, three hours later; the time it took for the influential Madame B . . . to vouch for the socialite Madame Alice Fayatt; and for the cabinet attaché Monsieur Sambrat, from Vichy, to vouch for his nephew, the industrialist Charles Sambrat. As they emerged from the Saint-Augustin barracks, by some miracle they came upon a carriage that picked them up and took them to the rue de Rivoli.

Chapter Eleven

CHARLES HADN'T said a word throughout the return journey. He held Alice's hand in his own and whistled 'Pink cherry trees and white apple trees' to a lugubrious tempo, just as he had done five hours earlier! It had taken place all within five hours! Alice was in a daze, but nevertheless lucid enough to hold back Charles outside his bedroom, not letting go of his hand, and to make him follow her into her room and to hug him in the darkness, saying 'Please, let's go to sleep,' in a tender but imperious tone of voice. Imperious enough that he was at first able to obey her, and this he did, in spite of himself, for an hour. But also tender enough that he was able to disobey her as well, once his body had regained its self-confidence.

Dawn had already returned to the sky's blue-tinged white sheets a long time ago, and it was broad daylight when he woke her, or she pretended to wake and opened her eyes on Charles's eyes, which were once more full of wonder. He lay beside her, looking enquiringly at her; her grey-blue eyes in the half-light, her disarmed, scared but consenting eyes, her eyes that were vulnerable to everything, including pleasure, saw him, had seen him; they had seen Charles and agreed. He knew now that

[135]

he would one day give her real pleasure, he knew this and smiled with happiness because of it, rejoicing in advance. Charles was too fond of women to succumb to vanity in one respect in particular; he had never imagined that he could gratify Alice the very first time, nor indeed any other woman of any subtlety. He had been especially fearful of having to love Alice without ever being able to share 'that' with her, and without being able to talk about it with her. In the pre-war period moral standards had been greatly relaxed, and if it had become less scandalous for a woman to give herself to a casual lover, as Alice had given herself to him, it was still forbidden to talk about the pleasure 'afterwards', without being pompous or crude, two styles that he equally detested. As for failures, or semi-failures, they were neither acknowledged nor commented upon.

But Charles already knew that even if Alice perhaps didn't yet love him for 'that', she did in any case like making love. A wave of jealousy momentarily checked his conqueror's happiness, his crazy happiness, and filled him with gloom. Who else before him, who . . . ? In any case, he reassured himself fiercely, it wasn't Jerome who had pleasured her. There was scorn and maliciousness in this thought, but the idea that she might have moaned beneath Jerome's caresses seemed to him as grotesque and odious as it was improbable. Men were repulsive to Charles, as has already been said, and Jerome sooner than any other; Jerome, whom he had known since childhood, whom he knew too well, with his boniness, his tall body and his blond pelt. And all the successes his friend had managed to score – these were less numerous than his own, of course, but often more flattering – had failed to convince Charles of the contrary. Alice and Jerome together – to him this was unimaginable. As Alice with anyone else at all would have been unimaginable, but alas, here it wasn't the unimaginable that he came up against, but real life. From today the full implications of Alice's beauty and seductiveness, of her aptitude for pleasure, made his head spin in anger and confusion.

As for Alice, she realized that making Charles happy was just as bearable as it would be unbearable to make him – or Jerome for that matter – unhappy. Even more so.

Towards midday he found Alice's sleeping face turned towards him. His surprise instantly gave way to a flurry of happiness. There was a burst of adrenalin and bliss around his heart that made his blood rush through his arteries and veins, throb in his temples, his wrists, his neck – his blood that was so fluid and light this morning and yet had been so thick and unruly the day before, at the *Aiglon*.

As he lay stretched out on his back, with his eyes open, Charles counted and recounted the mouldings in the ceiling and arrived at the same uncertain result as the day before (a century ago) when he had spent that sad afternoon in the depths of despair, engaged in mechanical computations. Now he smiled at the suddenly benevolent ceiling, a ceiling that once more resembled his destiny, at last. He would have fallen into a happy sleep again if Alice, who was surfacing from sleep and beating her eyelashes against his naked shoulder, hadn't suddenly dissuaded him. All at once she sat up in bed, and gave him such a frightened look that, although he was also anxious, Charles couldn't help laughing.

'Yes!' he said, not really daring to look at her. 'Yes, we're in the same bed.' He had opted at the last moment for 'we' as the most neutral form of expression, instead of saying '*you* are in *my* bed', or '*I* am in *your* bed', two equally inappropriate formulations of this unnecessary statement of the obvious. For a long while she said nothing, and Charles panicked. Was she looking at him

[137]

in astonishment? Had she been as drunk as all that yesterday? Did she hate him for it? Did he disgust her? Was she disgusted with herself? Had he done something dreadful? All these questions were jostling in his mind until Alice's warm silky mass of hair fell onto his face, a soft unexpected curtain that paradoxically announced, as it came down, a continuation of their story, a second act. He clasped his hands round Alice's back.

Later, in one of those moments of moral tranquillity that accompany physical fulfilment, when one feels closest to the other person but also most free, in one of those rare moments when the mind seems to share the wisdom and long-term intuitiveness of the body, and one can actually touch the body of one's beloved without turmoil, devotion or heartbreak, but with a strange sympathy, Charles had the courage, or the lack of affectation, to talk to Alice of his very recent terror. 'I thought that I should have cleared off into my room afterwards,' he said, 'that I shouldn't have stayed and imposed my desires and my presence on you.'

He spoke to her nonchalantly, constantly turning over Alice's forearm and hand in his own hands, bending the joints, studying the play of muscles, the pattern of veins, all this a delight to his sudden objectivity, which he thought he had acquired once and for all. Alice didn't make any attempt to withdraw her hand. She herself looked at her own wrist as though it were some alien object.

'You were wrong,' she said, 'there's no shame in wanting, desiring, daring. It's not desiring, or wanting, or daring any more that's shameful. It's not excessiveness that's horrible, it's inadequacy. "Too much" are far more decent words than "not enough". Believe me, I know, I lived in terms of "not enough" for a very long time and I'm still ashamed of it.'

[138]

He fell back and closed his eyes. It seemed to him that Alice was talking to him for the first time as a human being and not as a seducer. There passed from him to her a feeling of friendship, a friendship he was horribly mistrustful of after making love, but whose tenderness he could not shun this time.

'Why do you say that to me?' he said. 'Who are you thinking of? Are you thinking of Jerome, or your husband, that Gerhardt of yours?'

'I was thinking of Gerhardt,' she said.

She sat on the bed, bent her knees and clasped them in her arms, then rested her head on her arms. Like that, she resembled a child. As in the country, he would have liked to butter her bread for her, tell her to forget everything else, to forget the men she hadn't loved, or hadn't loved enough, or who had loved her too much – what difference did it make! – the men who hadn't made her happy, whose own unhappiness she now took pleasure in shouldering responsibility for.

'Tell me,' he said. 'Tell me everything, I want you to tell me everything. As soon as you came into my house, I wanted you to tell me everything, I wanted to stop you talking and make you talk at the same time. Talk to me, Alice, I beg you, talk to me. And may I use "*tu*" with you?'

'Yes, you may, you may do whatever you like with me,' she said smiling enigmatically. 'But don't be annoyed if I say "*vous*" when I'm talking to you. I wouldn't want to hurt you, Charles, never. It's essential that you know that. I don't want what happened with Gerhardt to happen again.'

'What happened with Gerhardt?' asked Charles, astonished by the clarity of his own voice. For right from the start he had hated Gerhardt, the fellow who'd had the gall, the cowardice to run away, to leave a country overrun with Germans, Nazis, bastards, and desert his wife to go and settle down in a cottage on the banks of the Mississippi, no doubt . . .

'What happened,' said Alice, 'was that I stopped loving him and he loved me. I think I told you,' she said, using "*vous*", then corrected herself, 'I told you what was happening to him outside the house. One evening . . . one evening I saw Gerhardt come home. He wrenched the door open, closed it with a kick, and then went straight to the kitchen. He tore open the door of the cupboard that had the dustbin in it, and opened his briefcase over it, his doctor's bag, and threw away everything inside, it, everything – the syringes, the medicines, the stethoscope, the pressure gauge, everything, everything there was inside it – he threw it all into the dustbin, in with the vegetable peelings and rubbish, without a word, with no explanation. And then he went into his bedroom and left the bag open and overturned in the corridor outside his door. I don't think he could take it any more. I think he was waiting with some kind of hope for his last operation, which he was supposed to perform the following month, and after that, he knew, they would send him, in turn, to his death. To tell the truth, I believe he hoped to die,' she said again.

'And then?' said Charles.

'And then Jerome arrived. He took charge of everything. I don't know whether you're aware of it or not, Charles, but Jerome has known since 1936 or '37 about everything that's been going on in Germany, about everything the Nazis have been doing since 1933, and he's been risking his life to save people, to get them over the border, to spare them the worst. More often than not they're Jews, of course. He happened to know Gerhardt, they'd met in Bayreuth, I believe, and he was very fond of him. Well, he persuaded Gerhardt to leave. He finally managed to persuade him. We left Vienna one night with false papers, in the most unremarkable, unromantic way in the world; and Gerhardt managed to get to Lisbon, and then America.'

'And you didn't go with him?' asked Charles, transforming what was evidently true into an indiscreet question, though it no longer occurred to Alice not to answer it. The fact that she'd one day accused Charles of anti-Semitism placed such a burden of guilt on her that she now couldn't blame him for anything else. In her eyes he had proved to be innocent, once and for all. 'No,' she said, 'I didn't want to go with him, we were in the process of getting divorced. In fact, that's why . . .'

She stopped and it was Charles who went on in a dreamy voice:

'Yes, that's why he emptied his bag into the dustbin, all by himself, leaving his bag in the corridor. Of course. You didn't love him any more?'

'I didn't love him . . . it's not that I didn't love him any more, I didn't love anybody,' said Alice in a grief-stricken voice. 'It was mostly that I didn't like myself any more, and that's horrible, believe me. I'm well aware of what men think about women's nervous depressions. I'm well aware that it seems ridiculous when you're young and wealthy, when you're by no means ugly and married to someone you find attractive. I'm well aware that despair in cases like that is grotesque, but believe me . . .'

'But I do believe you!' exclaimed Charles, so quickly he made Alice jump. 'I believe every word of it! I didn't tell Jerome, but that uncle I mentioned to you, Antoine – you'll say that I'm always harking back to my uncle, whatever we talk about, that it's ridiculous, but I learnt a lot of things from him; and sometimes without his intending it – well, my uncle Antoine had the same thing, this nervous depression. And it was dreadful. I think in the end that's what killed him. After all, people don't die of bronchitis if they care about living. It just

[141]

came upon him one day. He "fell sad", as we say where I come from. He took no interest in anything any more, not his friends, or the weather, or hunting, and believe me, he was quite a huntsman. Quite a womanizer, too. And what's more he liked working!' he said regretfully, as though this quality had not been passed on to him hereditarily, and that this was a great shame. Then he went on:

'I know what that illness means, Alice, believe me. I saw him sitting in his armchair looking out of the window for hours on end. I saw him go to bed in despair and wake up in despair. And I couldn't do anything for him, nothing at all. I could hardly talk to him, I felt I was boring him, and yet I was the only person in the world that he loved. I saw him in torment, I saw him gently banging himself against a wall – gently because even hurting himself didn't interest him any more. That's what it's like, isn't it, you aren't even able to kill yourself? No, believe me, Alice, I know what it is. If there's one thing I fear in this world, it's that, not liking myself any more. Not that I'm particularly fond of myself,' he added very quickly, 'but I do let myself be, I do leave myself in peace and, from time to time, I would sooner make myself laugh.'

He had spoken with fervour and conviction, but it was in a low voice that he added, 'I know that I'm describing this illness very badly, and that I can't really understand what it's like without having suffered from it myself . . . but I thought it would be less painful for you . . . Even if I express myself badly, I swear to you, Alice, I don't find it absurd; I find it terrifying.'

He stopped. He actually felt rather absurd and clumsy, but he knew that he had been clumsy in exactly the right way. And in some confused way he felt proud and pleased with himself. He had the impression – an impression long since forgotten – of having done someone a good turn; and for all that he was used to doing this for his dogs and horses, for 'his people' as he would say, for his trees and meadows, he was unused to doing women a good turn. That's to say, what he used to call women before this one turned up, embodying something quite different from that vague term, that odd, almost intellectual entity. It was a mean image that he used to have of women, an image that had nothing to do with this being, who was at once light and heavy, and sniffling a little on his shoulder. Alice had fallen asleep again, or pretended to fall asleep, without commenting further on Charles's clinical description. But from time to time she pressed her half-open lips to his body and each time she did so he trembled with happiness, felt his skin quiver all over, just as the skin of a skittish horse quivers beneath the palm of a hand that really knows it, whose touch the horse enjoys.

He thought he must have dozed off for a moment, doubtless he did sleep for a few minutes, a few long minutes, for when he opened his eyes again she was again sitting in that childlike pose, with her black hair falling over her grey eyes, and she was blowing it out of her eyes with a funny tomboyish grimace that made her beauty more human, more fallible, more accessible.

'What are you thinking about?' he asked.

'I was thinking about you,' she replied without looking at him, and her unexpected, unhoped-for use of the familiar '*tu*' came as a shock to Charles, who'd used '*vous*'.

'What are you thinking about,' he said, echoing her term of intimacy.

'I was thinking about you with those Germans this morning,' she said. 'I was thinking about you . . .' And she started laughing, despite herself, like some schoolgirl.

'I was quite ludicrous,' said Charles. 'I thought that you would always see me like that, looking ridiculous and obscene, with my trousers crumpled round my ankles. What did you think? Tell me!' he added with sudden fury, and she stopped laughing, put her hand to Charles's face and kept it there, with her thumb on his cheek, her fingers behind his ear, and her nails buried in the roots of his hair.

'I thought you looked handsome,' she said. 'Your body was suntanned to your hips, you stood very straight; I found you very, very arousing, with your white skin looking like a pair of swimming trunks, and your brown thighs. And if it hadn't been for '*mein capitaine*' I would have whistled in admiration. And anyway, I did show my admiration, didn't I?'

'That's certainly true,' said Charles, half-shocked, half-delighted, 'it's true, that Kraut couldn't believe his eyes either. Was that when you decided to . . . to . . . ?'

'No, no,' said Alice very quickly and very untruly, 'it was while we were dancing in that nightclub that I made up my mind.'

She had fallen back on the bed, and had a reserved, distant air about her; doubtless she didn't take seriously all of Charles's prudish ways, and this annoyed him. She had been so spiritually removed from this bed they'd shared, and now she seemed so at ease in it. In Charles's experience 'nice' women were quite the contrary – as provocative beforehand as they were shy afterwards; they would re-cast their timid suitors into cynical seducers after the very first night. 'I wonder what you'll think of me now?' was one of the questions Charles had heard most often in his life, and one to which he never replied. Alice didn't ask this question, would never ask it, had never asked it. Perhaps this was a matter of background, but in this instance the one she came from was preferable to his own.

'I'm hungry,' she said, opening her eyes again. 'What can they be doing with their dishwatery tea and their

[144]

white bread that tastes of cardboard?' But someone was already knocking at the door, and Charles called out 'Come in' in a haughty voice, pulling the sheets over Alice's shoulders and face with a fierce tug. The poor boy put down his tray without daring to look at the bed and left the way he had entered, looking neither left nor right.

In the end, they found their breakfast very enjoyable; as was the white wine the embittered (though in the end more avaricious than embittered) concierge had obtained for them, for a small fortune, at about three o'clock, along with some indefinable sandwiches; as was the other bottle they drank that evening. Their half-empty, forgotten glasses reflected the slanting rays of the setting sun and the crumbs scattered in their sheets added to their well-being. They went to sleep very late, without having got up, or even thought of getting up, for without having said anything about it either, they both knew they would have to go home the next day. And like two people who'd met on a railway station, they spoke to each other only in the present tense, and never used the future.

And so it was that in Charles's memory Paris ceased to be the capital city of pleasures and became that of happiness. Instead of sunny days, café terraces, countless women, chestnut trees, orchestras, dawns, a whole city, Paris evoked nothing but a hotel room in the semi-darkness and the profile of a single woman; the heart is a poor tourist.

Chapter Twelve

THEIR TRAIN didn't leave until midday, but they followed Jerome's instructions and got to the Gare de Lyons at ten thirty – not without some difficulty. They had dropped off to sleep very late, in a state of exhaustion, having had their fill of each other, or so they thought. But later on, and then even later, the never-satiated animal called love lying crouched in their bodies and nerves had woken them up again, and again driven them towards each other, into embraces that neither one nor the other felt responsible for instigating.

With trembling legs, dry mouths and thumping hearts, they had wandered and roamed in a dream along platforms, then along the corridors of the train, before leaving, in the luggage rack of a compartment chosen at random, a case full of false documents intended for Jerome. The rule was to put the case anywhere, and they had followed the rule with almost equal obedience and remorse.

Now they had taken refuge in the sinister, dirty station buffet, had ordered two chicory coffees and each was looking with amazement and compassion at the pale, crumpled ghost of their impassioned nocturnal love-making now in front of them. From right at the back of this buffet, where it was dark and deserted, they saw in the distance, beneath the glass roof at the end of the platforms, a golden, rustic, alien sun burst forth and hold sway, a sun more evocative of memories of their distant childhood than of their immediate future. Yet they would soon be travelling towards this very sun, towards green countryside, summer, grass and rivers. Very soon, in a few minutes. But they weren't thinking of this; as they sat behind their luggage, still as night birds, scared and incredulous, struck rigid at their table, their memories brimmed over with all-powerful images in tune with their feelings: flashes of sheets, bodies, faces, sighs, dark shadows and lightning blazes of pleasure. Their memories, become things of the night, made null and void and unimaginable their present, their future, their imagination and reason – even the sun shining over there.

Neither of them had mentioned Jerome's name, but the voice over the loudspeaker announcing that their train would be delayed by more than an hour seemed to both of them the voice of an angel of mercy.

There were twelve of them in a compartment intended for six, and the train seemed to be racked with some kind of spasmodic lumbago that both Alice and Charles were eternally grateful for. Nevertheless, partly because he couldn't speak to Alice, partly because of his boredom, Charles began to ponder seriously on his own intentions. What should he do? Was it up to him to speak to Jerome, or to her? He couldn't imagine himself taking Jerome aside as soon as he got back and talking to him, man to man. Man to man! What an expression! And what was he to say to him? 'I'm in love with your mistress and she's a little in love with me too, at least she allows me to love her.' This solution, which he might readily have opted for, and even preferred a month earlier, in his rustic or Lyonnaise vaudeville days, now

[148]

seemed to him ridiculous and crass. Of course, it was up to Alice to speak to him; and that must seem awful to her. Charles could understand how she must feel; now the happy rival and no longer the scorned suitor, he became the fraternal friend again, he rediscovered the affection and compassion that Jerome and his unhappy love affairs had always inspired in him. In Charles's imagination Jerome's destiny was a kind of straight path – very straight and illuminated and melancholy. In a way, Jerome had a talent for unhappiness and the fact that this time it was Charles himself who was the bearer of his unhappiness was just a twist of fate – an unfortunate twist of fate, of course, but a twist of fate nonetheless. In any case, with or without Charles, Jerome would not have kept Alice; first, because the women Jerome loved didn't stay with him; and also – though Charles didn't really put it to himself in so many words – because Alice wouldn't stay with anybody. This was an intuition that at times played havoc with Charles's mind, but it would quickly pass, and even disappear, the minute he smelt the fragrance of Alice's body on his own hand.

Charles told himself that he was taking back to Jerome the great love of his friend's life, the love he himself had just robbed him of, but he didn't feel in the least bit guilty; he felt he was only a witness, an onlooker, Alice's healer. There was just one thing he really feared: that remorse might spoil the early stages of their love affair, and their happiness born only yesterday. Thanks to a gap that appeared between two shoulders, a neck and a case, his eyes met Alice's. He gave her a reassuring wink of encouragement, which informed Alice of his state of mind better than any speech could have done. No, she mustn't count on Charles to fret and worry, or to put himself in Jerome's position. Charles was a born inno-cent, just as he was born with brown hair, and he would die innocent even if his hair had time to turn white as snow.

He didn't realize that she owed everything to Jerome, he didn't realize that Jerome had fallen madly in love with her at first sight and that he had pledged his whole life to her, even when she gave him no hope. It was Jerome who, for more than two years, had spent hours and hours watching over her, in Vienna, in Paris, on trains, in clinics, everywhere. It was Jerome who had listened to her, forgiven her, spoken to her, absolved her. It was Jerome who had looked after her as though she were a child, it was Jerome who had found for her husband a way to survive and for herself a reason for living. It was Jerome who had saved her, who had never asked anything of her, though she owed him everything, whose gratitude had been boundless when she had made him the modest, futile gift of her body. It was Jerome who had only ever thought of her own good, Jerome to whom she was going to do the greatest wrong anyone could possibly do him.

This was how Alice once again found herself a prisoner of principles. Her whole life had been nothing but a long battle, a stealthy, bitter struggle between conventions and her own nature. If it had been solely up to her, Alice wouldn't have said anything to Jerome. She would have granted him her body, lent it to him tenderly, absent-mindedly, affectionately, as she had done for the past six months, and she would have shared Charles's bed, bringing to it all the sensuality, curiosity, gaiety and even esteem that this man aroused in her. Jerome wouldn't have been plunged into despair, she wouldn't have suffered as a result, she wouldn't have felt guilty and life would have been harmonious. But it wasn't so easy! Neither of these supposedly tolerant, intelligent men – one a libertine and the other a humanist – would have tolerated this situation. Sharing her would have seemed an impossibility to them. How absurd it was! You couldn't share something or somebody unless the thing or person was yours, and they were both well aware that she didn't belong to either of them. You can never possess another human being. You might be attached to someone, and as a result that someone might be attached to you, for as long as your feeling for him lasts. But to think of possessing anyone! And yet Jerome and Charles, who were willing to share her regard, her tenderness and her affection, refused to share her body, as though her body were more important than her feelings. It was thanks to this absurd premise that she was going to have to hurt someone she cherished; it was through this sense of 'propriety' that she was going to be cruel.

Yes, her whole life had been nothing but pretence. It was out of curiosity and not out of love that she had taken her first lover. It was through ineptitude and ignorance that she had found herself pregnant by Gerhardt, not through any taste for motherhood. And it was to spare her family's feelings that she married him, not from any desire to share his life. It was by accident that she'd had a miscarriage, not by design or out of disgust. It was so as not to upset Gerhardt, and not because she loved him, that she went to live in Vienna. It was out of kindness, almost out of courtesy, and not out of sensuality, that she had taken a lover. It was because of her passion for life, a disappointed passion, that she had suffered that nervous depression. It was through cowardice and fear of hurting herself that she hadn't killed herself, and not because of any taste for life. It was out of horror of loneliness that she had allowed herself to be loved by Jerome, and not because she wanted to return his love. It was fear of America, of the unknown, that had made her remain where she was

[151]

and decide to join the Resistance, not courage or rebellion against Nazi brutality. And it was through tiredness that she had given herself to Jerome one evening, not through tenderness or by inclination. Ultimately, there was only one thing she had done naturally until now: slept with Charles, out of physical desire, because she found him attractive and his desire was infectious.

And it was because she still found him attractive, because he made her laugh and gave her confidence that she was going to stay with him. Yes, for the first time she was going to do something because it was what she wanted to do. She was going to leave Jerome for the sake of the pleasure it would give her to live with Charles – it wasn't just viciousness on her part. No, not that! The cruelty of what she was going to do made her turn pale, and she hated the society that forced this cruelty upon her, that declared all sharing to be monstrous. But so what if she was monstrous! Alice was a delicate, gentle woman, all her friends, her relations, her husband, her several lovers could swear to this without lying, but no one knew what incredible determination there was inside the little head perched on that dainty neck. Alice would never deliberately mislead anyone, or deceive herself, either about her feelings or her thoughts. And sometimes she would laugh at herself, coldly, against what she called her 'flaw', the pretentious naiveté that had already brought her to a state of despair all the more profound because it fed off itself, and only pleasure and laughter, the uncontrollable and the absurd, could escape its vigilance. Fortunately for her, Alice had in her veins some Irish and Hungarian blood, which offered her the two escapes – pleasure and laughter – more often than to other women; if she knew which inclination she was giving way to, they were varied enough for her not to get bored – as long as she didn't destroy herself.

*

The train was now travelling at a regular speed; they would be crossing the demarcation line in an hour and a half. The announcement had passed from carriage to carriage, from compartment to compartment, as if the whole train had been one long travelling gaol, with all the murmurings and tension of prisons. The travellers fidgeted, checked their watches and bags, looked at each other with new eyes; theirs was no longer the weary, exasperated look of individuals crowded by their fellowmen but the anxious, mistrustful and puritanical look of individuals whom these same fellowmen are in danger of compromising. Charles, who had been standing for two hours, clinging to the luggage rack, resting against Alice's knees, was amazed to see the faces beneath him turn impassive. And it came as no surprise when Alice signalled to him to bend down, by pinching his arm.

'Charles,' she whispered, 'I'd like you . . . you' (she corrected herself, using the familiar pronoun) 'to go and look in the other compartment, you know, where we left the case, to see what the other passengers are like, you know . . . if anything were to happen . . .'

Yes, Charles knew. He knew everything that Alice's voice implied, and he smiled at her in tenderness and amusement, although exhausted beforehand by the mere thought of getting through the human mêlée packed into the corridors that lay between him and the suitcase in question. But without even attempting to argue about it, he launched himself into the fray. It took him more than three-quarters of an hour to get there and back, and Alice was deathly white by the time he returned, looking dishevelled but reassuring. He bent down and whispered in his turn: 'I had a good look, and as far as I could see – and I mean just that – there weren't any Jews or small children or anyone who might be in the Resistance in that compartment. It reeked more of black-marketeers. But,' he added with a smile, 'since there was one fat dairywoman with a kindly face who perhaps gives bread to the poor at Christmas, I did what was required.'

With a burst of laughter he brought his right hand to the fore, having kept it behind his back until then; he had the suitcase hanging from it. He heaved the case up onto the disparate pile in the luggage rack and looked at Alice. She had a grateful smile on her face that made him feel awkward.

'In any case, you would have sent me back again,' he said, laughing, 'and it's a hellish trip to make.'

'All the same, you were lucky to find it again,' said Alice, also speaking out loud, and their travelling companions, who were at first intrigued and suspicious, but then reassured by this laughter, turned their eyes away from this disturbing suitcase so late in arriving. Alice took Charles's hand that was hanging at the level of her face and pressed her cheek to it. As he stood over her with his eyes shut, it was Charles's mad hope, for one moment, that he would be shot, together with her, at the next stop. And yet . . . a wish to die alongside anyone at all was extremely rare with him . . . He could remember having formulated such a wish on only one occasion, when the haberdasher's daughter had ditched him for a pupil in the sixth form on the same day as his fourteenth birthday. How odd! It would never have occurred to him that happiness might bring you to the same reveries as sorrow.

It was staggeringly hot at the demarcation line and the German officer who opened the door of the compartment pulled his face in disgust at the sight of the good French citizens all crammed in together, sweating and sweltering in seats of a dubious grey. He inspected everyone's papers without batting an eyelid. He was a little dark-haired man who looked like a Southerner, and the fact that he wasn't the perfect Aryan type must have made him aggressive, because he shouted his head off several times. He almost tore Charles's pass out of his hands, made a few jokes in German as he pointed to Alice with his chin, studied Charles, who had no trouble getting into a muddle over some story about a secretary – a story that was too obviously untrue not to be plausible – and with a ribald, scornful smile, to everyone's relief he left the compartment. No one noticed how tense and uneasy Alice and Charles looked. On the journey to Paris they would have laughed merrily and without any embarrassment over these crude jokes, but now the jokes sounded to them like so many obscenities.

So the train set off once more and very quickly started the same performance all over again. It hiccoughed, stopped, pitched this way and that, restarted, stopped again, and went on doing this all night long, and apparently the engine drivers and the guard could do nothing about it. They didn't get to Valence station until dawn.

Jerome was waiting for them outside, leaning against a plane tree, and when he saw them he started running towards them, like some gangling student, which slightly disturbed Charles's spirit and his memory. Fortunately, Jerome had remained discreet and, with his friend looking on, it was Alice's forehead that he kissed. He looked so radiant that Charles's mood darkened. And yet he was happy; he felt a strange happiness, a new happiness, at the thought of seeing his meadows, his house and his dogs again. He suddenly felt a genuine relief, the relief of feeling secure again, and of having brought Alice back to this security, safe and sound. And it was a curious feeling, since he had never for one moment had the impression he was facing the least danger, except on a purely emotional level.

The train was already pulling out, rapidly for once,

[155]

when he remembered the case. He manged to jump on and get off again without coming to any harm, but his heart was beating wildly, and his legs felt watery. He certainly wasn't getting any younger, he thought happily. He came back brandishing his spoils in triumph, holding the case at arm's length as he made his way towards Jerome, who was signalling caution at him, but who had taken advantage of his absence to slip his right arm round Alice's shoulders. All of a sudden Charles brusquely held out the case to him, which unlocked Jerome's embrace and took him by surprise. He raised his eyebrows questioningly.

'I'm sorry, I'm dead beat,' said Charles, 'really dead beat. It was a hellish journey.'

'And apart from that?' said Jerome. 'Apart from that?'

His eyes were merry and he looked so intensely relieved that Charles turned away, suddenly horrified at himself. For the first time he felt remorseful; it was his first moment of remorse, but it was intense.

Chapter Thirteen

THE OLD CAR was waiting for them nearby, but pointing towards the road, just as in detective films, thought Charles absentmindedly. He was going to take the wheel when, to his great surprise, Alice slipped in before him.

'Let me drive this machine for once, Charles. After all, I've never driven it.'

Somewhat astounded, the two men got in, Charles in front and Jerome in the back with the suitcases, and Alice drove off brilliantly. She didn't even grind the gears, noted Charles, amused and astonished.

'I used to have a Talbot Lago,' she said, laughing and taking a corner rather sharply to avoid a cyclist. 'I even won a race at La Baule when I was nineteen or twenty. At that time it was rare for women to drive. My goodness, that seems a long time ago, it's terrifying . . .'

'Apart from the Talbot Lago, you don't have any more recent memories, Alice?' asked Jerome in a purring tone of voice.

'But of course,' said Charles without giving Alice time to reply. 'But of course, we've got lots of exciting things to tell you. That suitcase is full of false passports. We put it in a different carriage from our own and then Alice was afraid they might shoot the poor people travelling with it. So I had to go and fetch it. You can't

imagine all the trouble she's caused me,' he added play-
fully, ingenuously giving a terribly clumsy tap to Alice's
arm on the steering wheel. She jumped and the car
swerved.

We've made a good start, thought Charles, we've
made a really good start.

Providently, Elisa had prepared a real meal for them –
real omelette, real saucisson, and some real red wine,
followed by real coffee. It was all served on the terrace
and Charles couldn't have felt more content. The wind
softly shook the leaves of the plane trees over their heads,
the blue-white dawn sky was turning to pale blue, that
pale blue common to all hot summers, and the lazy
jogging of the dog Blitz along the gravel path made a
delightful sound. Alice and Jerome, who were equally
silent, also seemed to appreciate the beauty of the hour
as much as the saucisson. Charles glanced at each of
them – first, a furtive glance at Alice, stretched out on
the chaise-longue with her eyes closed, and a second
affectionate, compassionate glance at Jerome, whose eyes
were open and focused on the end of the meadow. Oh
no, the forthcoming explanation wasn't going to be any
fun for Alice!

Meanwhile, Charles considered himself to be behaving
perfectly, being as distant and remote with Alice as he
remembered having been attentive and restless before
their departure. He talked of Paris abstractedly, as if
they had been there to visit the Eiffel Tower, the Arc de
Triomphe and Les Invalides. He didn't even mention
their subversive activities because that topic, of a
historico-sentimental nature, effectively belonged to
Jerome and Alice, and not to him. The Resistance was
their baby, it was the starting-point, the *raison d'être* of
the couple they had once been – this at least was what
Charles liked to tell himself.

To be frank, when it came to the point, he had to admit that if Jerome had launched into one of his speeches about Marshal Pétain, France and the occupying forces again, he would have found it very difficult to contradict him. He would not have replied with the same irony or the same phlegm as before. He remembered all too well their arrival in Paris, a sinister Paris of deserted streets. As for that famous night of theirs, though he remained dazzled by the outcome, he still had a horrified memory of what had preceded it. He couldn't contradict Jerome and Alice – not any more – because they were right. But he didn't want to add grist to their mills – and especially not to Alice's. Everything that might lead her – a delicate woman who'd become a creature of flesh and blood for him – into the dangers he now knew to be of the most concrete nature was to be firmly repelled. His own imagination, which, like his memory, had been deliberately optimistic ever since the end of hostilities, was no longer so. He might have been an aggressive brat until the age of twenty-five, but it had been quite a while since Charles had been involved in a physical fight. Above all, it had been quite a while since he'd been given a brutal and savage hammering by men in uniform. The idea of Alice's soft, white, warm body being touched, attacked or manhandled by that sadistic, crude army rabble was so appalling that he had to look up at her and examine her to prove to himself that she was intact. He suddenly felt silly, and was obliged to look away or cast a sweeping glance over her before fixing his eyes on some particular point in the fence, or the tablecloth or his own hands.

Yet Jerome looked calm, he spoke easily, unspiritedly, with that phlegmatic air of his, the air of an Englishman, young or old, that Charles had so often criticized at school. For that matter, it would be a good thing if the English aristocrat in him gave way to the partisan and lover, and he asked some questions, so that they could give him some answers, some truthful answers, however brutal these might be. For Charles could see very clearly that Alice wouldn't speak to him unless she was constrained and forced to. Though she was incapable of lying to him, she would be incapable of telling him the truth right out of the blue – and yet she would have to, since Charles was intending to spend the night in her arms.

He was hesitating, as he rocked in his chair. All Charles's idleness, all his horror of dramas rebelled against this scene to come, but for once the exacting nature of his love was greater than his laziness; and remembering the number of times he had let his mistresses go, to return temporarily to their husbands, if only to avoid their shouting and accusations, Charles felt half-amused by and half-ashamed of the quiet, peaceable and accommodating lover he had found it so easy to be all his life. And he was just as surprised at his use of the past tense, which he now invariably used – though since only recently – when talking about himself.

'I'm entitled to an account of what happened. Now,' said Jerome suddenly. 'A detailed account. For a start, who gave you that badge of honour on your eye, my poor Charles? Was it Alice?'

'No, not at all,' exclaimed Charles with expansive gestures of denial that were completely pointless. 'It was a German, or rather, a group of Germans.'

'Because you had a fight with some Germans?' asked Jerome in an easygoing tone of voice. 'Well, well, well, that must make a colourful story . . .'

'You've hit on exactly the right word for it, Jerome,' said Alice with a smile. 'I'm sure Charles is going to tell it as if it were a question of a couple of drunks getting some rough handling from the police, I'm convinced he will. You begin the story, Charles, I shan't interrupt you, but I'll give my version afterwards.'

'Out of the question!'

'Why?' said Jerome, 'could it be that you're afraid?'

'Me, afraid? Afraid of what?' protested Charles in a shrill voice. 'What makes you think I should be afraid? If you'd heard those two fellows insulting Alice, you'd have done the same.'

'But which fellows?' asked Jerome, more and more intrigued.

Alice cut in. 'Charles means the two SS men who took us to the *Kommandantur* in Place Saint-Augustin for interrogation.'

Jerome leapt up, suddenly pale.

'You went to the *Kommandantur?* But you've told me nothing about that, why haven't you told me? What happened?

'Charles is going to tell you all about it. Go on, Charles, be brave!' said Alice.

'I'm quite willing to begin the story, but I shall stop at the point where we came out of the *Kommandantur,*' said Charles firmly. 'Alice will tell you the rest,' he added.

And the insanity of his words, his craziness, seemed so enormous to Alice and to himself that they looked at each other, stunned, unblinking and on the verge of laughter.

'Well, this is what happened,' Charles began painfully. 'I promised Alice I would take her dancing, you know, to . . . to . . . to amuse her, and I asked the concierge at the hotel . . . you know that hotel where we used to go, or at least I used to go in the past, don't you? Don't you know it? The Dandy in the rue de Rivoli. Yes, you do, I gave you the telephone number.'

'Listen,' said Jerome, 'don't confuse things. What did you ask the concierge?'

[161]

'Nothing. Yes, I did . . . I asked him for the address of a place where we could go dancing. We went to the *Aiglon*, in the rue de Berri, it's the latest fashionable nightclub. It was packed with all kinds of people – Germans, even generals, businessmen . . . there was even a playwright and two actors, isn't that so, Alice?' he asked her.

She was displaying an air of inattentiveness, a vaguely bored look that annoyed Charles.

'Yes, yes, that's true, there were some famous faces,' she admitted.

'Well, we danced,' said Charles, 'what was it we danced, as a matter of fact? We danced to the tunes they were playing.'

'Actually,' Alice intervened, 'I think we were more like Millet's dutiful tillers of the soil than Fred Astaire and Ginger Rogers. At the beginning of the evening Charles made us plough our way across the dance floor until we'd covered a good three or four kilometres, without a moment's pause, and . . .'

'You're exaggerating,' said Charles, 'we weren't just covering ground the whole time. I made up for it afterwards.'

'Yes, thank God, he had a drop to drink,' she said – this for Jerome's benefit – 'he had a drop to drink and allowed himself a few variations, a few detours in his itinerary. Then at curfew we went back to the hotel – still on foot, to continue our training. And that was when we ran into the Germans, or rather the Germans pounced on us. Please go on, Charles, I said I wouldn't butt in!'

'That woman is not to be relied upon!' Charles said to Jerome. 'After all, you know me, you know that I'm not at all bad at dancing! Don't you remember, I was in the finals of that dancing competition . . . what was it now, that dance thing at the Pantheon? Do you remember?'

'Listen,' said Jerome harshly. 'I don't care whether you danced well or badly, what interests me is the story about the Germans, so get on with it.'

'What about it? You know it all!' said Charles in exasperation. 'You know it all! We were arrested, we were taken to the *Kommandantur*, we were asked who we were, where we came from, everything! I said we'd come from the *Aiglon*, that we were staying in the rue de Rivoli. They asked to see our papers, Alice got hers out, which proved she was Jewish, or at least not that she was Jewish but that her husband was and she wasn't. And then they indulged in a few jokes – more Goebbels' style of humour than Sacha Guitry's – about the Jewish race. And,' he very quickly added, 'and afterwards they let us go. At least, someone had to vouch for us and say that we were good French citizens and that we therefore adored the German race. That's all.'

'And who vouched for you?' asked Jerome.

'Well, Madame Somebody-or-other vouched for Alice and my uncle Sambrat vouched for me – the one in Vichy, the one who's an attaché to Laval's cabinet, I believe. You know, that idiot Uncle Didier? We went shooting with him once, don't you remember? On top of everything, he sprays shot all over the place!'

'Alice,' said Jerome, 'Alice, he's never going to get to the point, will you explain?'

'Right, I'll start at the beginning again. After the *Aiglon*, we went back via the Place de la Concorde, and on the corner of the rue Boissy d'Anglais we found ourselves in a porchway in the company of a terrorist the Germans were looking for. They saw him with us, thought we were his accomplices and took us away to check our identities. One of them saw my papers, made some crude remark about my weakness for Gerhardt and

[163]

my taste for circumcised men. Charles lost his temper and went for them – as though we were dealing with a bunch of honest-to-God cops. They beat him senseless and we went back to the hotel. That's all. And to have done with all the trivial details, I must make the point that, having drunk five or six cognacs, Charles finally thawed. And we danced the *paso doble*, the tango, the fandango and the waltz in admirable style, to the cheering of the crowd.'

Alice was staring at Charles as she said these words, trying to make him understand that he was to leave as quickly as possible, that he was to go away, that she was going to speak now, that he mustn't be there; but he was looking at her, looking at Jerome, with an air of relief and self-satisfaction, the air of a man who hasn't put his foot in it. He is incredible, she thought, he's crazy. What a simpleton. She found him really very attractive.

'Right, and after the details, as you call them Alice, after the *Kommandantur*, as you put it, Charles, what happened? What is it you don't want to tell me, Charles?'

Charles eyes turned towards Alice.

She murmured, 'What I learned yesterday morning, Jerome, which doesn't concern Charles. Would you please leave us?' she asked Charles, who did as he was asked, and heard Alice's voice behind him, a low trembling voice, pronounce some names that were unknown to him, and yet seemed strangely familiar and friendly – 'Tolpin, Faroux and Dax' – just as familiar and friendly as her sentence, when concluded, seemed cruel – 'Tolpin, Faroux and Dax have been shot,' said Alice sadly, tenderly, as she might have said, 'I confess I have always loved you.'

Charles was exhausted and fell asleep almost at once. Alice tossed and turned for a long time before managing

[164]

to do so. As for Jerome, who had spent three ghastly days waiting for them, and was just as exhausted as they were, he went and stretched out under the poplar that had been his favourite since childhood.

But today he no longer saw the thousand little green leaves glinting and dancing in the sun, promising him every happiness. He felt relieved and sickened. Relieved since Alice had returned safe and sound, and sickened by this relief; for now he knew, she had told him, he was certain of what he had already sensed: Tolpin, Faroux and Dax were dead, shot. That carrot-top Tolpin, with his frizzy hair, his smile, that face of his that was all red the whole time; and Faroux, who was so clumsy, so guarded, so decent and well bred that you couldn't even imagine his being arrested; and Dax, with that air of sovereignty he had, a short man's way of cutting bigger men down to size. These three human beings, three men he had met by chance – because they had the same notion of life he had, the same certainty that some things were impermissible – these three men had been condemned to death and executed.

And here he was, alive! Their boss, as it were – in as much as he could feel like a boss – and here he was, sprawled under a tree, watching the poplar leaves and rejoicing because his mistress, that beautiful mistress of his, had come back to him unharmed. And most of all, most of all, he – honest, sensible, responsible Jerome – was tormented a thousand times more by this woman's possible betrayal of him than by the certain death of his friends. For though their deaths overwhelmed him with sadness, despair and a manly sorrow beyond repair – for of course he would never forget Tolpin, Faroux and Dax – it was with a proud grief that his own image would have a place among theirs in his memory. On the other hand, it was with a dreadful throbbing pain, a dishonourable pain – because it was tainted with doubts

[165]

and suspicions and baseness – that he would later think of Alice and Charles. Those three brief moments – first in the car, then on the stairs, and finally in the drawing room – those three brief moments (and not, of course, the moments when Charles thought he had betrayed himself), those three brief moments when he had had a very cursory intuition of a new physical complicity between them . . . now that the two of them were no longer there and he no longer sought to amass or dismiss the evidence, those three moments multiplied tenfold.

He turned over onto his stomach and buried his face in the grass, beating the inert, warm, fragrant earth with his fist, violently; the earth that had always rejected him. Again he was sure of it, he was convinced of it, Alice and Charles had slept together in Paris, they had betrayed him, she had been unfaithful, they were happy, they were attractive to each other. And Charles had given Alice the pleasure he himself had never managed to give her. That 'good sort' Charles, that fool, that skirt-chaser, had succeeded in wresting from this woman, a thousand times more sensitive and intelligent than he was, the cries that Jerome himself had so long waited and hoped for. But was it true that there were 'ladies' men' and women ready to believe these ladies' men? Was it true that a woman like Alice could fall into such a low, burlesque, disgusting trap as the one set by Charles?

And what's more, she was going to talk to him, she was going to tell him the truth, she was going to say, 'I'm terribly sorry, Jerome, but it was a physical thing. You're the one I really love, the one I care about and understand, the one I feel good with; with Charles it's nothing but a sensual attraction. All that is of no importance, let's be friends, Jerome.' Was she stupid enough, cruel enough to imagine that it was her mind, her soul, her sensitivity that he especially wanted? Was she

[166]

unaware that, for him as for any man, it was what was of earth and clay in a woman, her blood, her skin, her flesh that mattered first and foremost, more than anything else? Was she unaware that if the body without the heart was not paradise, the heart without the body was hell? Was she unaware that while she was sleeping he had sometimes sobbed with rage and despair to see her looking so sweet and peaceful and trusting in his arms? Was she unaware that, at thirty years of age, he had actually pleasured some women and that he could distinguish between pleasure and affection in their faces and in their bodies?

Or did she think he was stupid, a cold, inexperienced fool? Oh God! He clenched his hands round the grass, tried to dig into the earth with his chin, his nose, his forehead; he beat his cheek against the ground. Oh, he would have given anything at all – his head, ten years, twenty years of his life – to hear that cry, if only once, Alice's cry of love! Once, just once! He felt he would do anything for that! And it was with a heaving of his stomach, a spasm that was like a feeling of sickness – only it rose not in his throat but in his whole body – that he turned over onto his back, then onto his side, with his knees tucked under his chin, his head in his arms, with both hands covering his face as though, in his anger and disgust, he wanted to hide the sight of it from whomsoever, and since there wasn't anybody there, to hide it as well from a fierce, stupid God he did not in any case believe in.

And through its very excess, his pain subsided. Perhaps his memory unconsciously reminded him that he had in the past expounded on those words of Nietzsche: 'It's not doubt but certainty that leads to madness.' And he heard his own voice again, a voice that had for a moment been blocked out and which was saying to him, 'Now then, Jerome, poor Jerome, here you are in

[167]

a foetal position! The famous foetal position!' And not being able to go on suffering like this, his mind – seeking everywhere for some tranquillizer, some remedy, something to eliminate this mortal pain – his mind could find only one recourse: doubt. He began to breathe more regularly. He began quite simply to breathe again. Oh, but upon my word, he was going mad, he was turning into an idiot! What was the meaning of this hysterical fit? Doubtless it was the shock of learning of the death of his friends; he had taken the news very badly. It was his sorrow and anguish and remorse at not having been with them. It had also been the dread that Alice might be arrested in Paris. It was his insomnia for the last three days that had put him into this state of impassioned frenzy. He had too much imagination, it was a weakness of his, a weakness that was all the more horrible in that it functioned especially in misfortune. Though his memory tended to be cheerful, to remember the good times, he only ever imagined the worst: always.

There was a person within him ready to be seduced, and charmed, who wanted to laugh and be confiding. But there was also another person, someone gloomy and distant, a tormented soul . . . And this duo had always been there, ever since birth. Only now he had the impression that this second person was getting the upper hand; and worse, he had a growing feeling that it was this second person, this pessimist, who was right. Unlike Charles, Jerome had never known how to slide down the slippery slope called happiness; he had always felt lame. Really, he was disabled, and the war allowed him to hide his disability. Jerome knew this, and simultaneously feared it and hoped it was so; it was only at the foot of the stake, when his body had been shattered and his soul was elsewhere, that he would rejoin his human brothers. All of the rest of the time would be spent chasing an image of himself, a cartoon image, of a happy Jerome. The only instances when life had seemed to gush forth like milk or alcohol were those he owed to Charles, his opposite and his brother. And perhaps his rival.

Chapter Fourteen

So IT WAS only after two hours of insomnia that Alice had drifted off to sleep. She was aroused seven hours later by Charles's car horn. Having slept peacefully from the moment his head touched the pillow, Charles had woken pretty early to go and make a tour of his factory. Hoping vaguely that Alice would have talked to Jerome, he was faced with the disappointment on his return of being able to see even from the gate that her shutters were still closed. And now he was waking her up with long bursts of his horn, for which he found an absurd excuse almost as soon as he got out of the car.

'Elisa,' he shouted, 'Elisa, I shall end up by running over these wretched birds if they go on throwing themselves under my car! What makes the poor creatures so desperate?'

In a reflex action that was still unconscious, Alice had leapt out of bed and rushed to the window. Half amused and half angry, she watched Charles waving his arms about in front of the car, and in front of an alarmed Elisa, who was casting reproachful looks at her chickens – though these were peacefully assembled in the court-yard – and scolding them undeservedly. Alice watched her lover through the shutters, gazing at his black hair and his long shadow in the setting sun, and was amazed by the sense of familiarity, the impression of being used to each other that she already felt with him.

'Do you think this fine weather is going to last?' Charles asked poor dumbfounded Elisa at the top of his voice. It was the first time Charles had ever asked such a ludicrous question – the sky being, from east to west, an absolutely perfect, limpid blue. She didn't realize that he wanted some excuse to look up, to see whether Alice was behind the shutters. He was behaving like a guilty man; ever since their arrival he had been affecting airs of innocence that would have set anybody thinking. He was going to such a lot of trouble to look innocent and all for nothing, since Jerome would have to know.

After all, she said to herself, turning towards the dressing table, what else had she herself done since arriving except be evasive, silent, to deceive Jerome a little longer? But her reflection in the mirror was not at all an image of remorse; her skin was pink, a little suntanned, her eyes looked bigger and were shining, and despite herself, she had a mocking expression on her face that made her look ten years younger. She was amazed, and amazed at her amazement. It was a good long time since she had last looked at herself in a mirror, or been amused by the beneficial effects on her face of sensuality. She smiled at herself for a moment and then felt appalled, for she imagined Jerome's face when she spoke to him in an hour or two – three at the most. She imagined the face of the man who loved her, her friend, a face that was so vulnerable beneath its calm, cold exterior. That face would become distorted, its features twisted, the mouth would tremble, everything that he was or had become through application, Jerome's very being, his generosity, confidence, steadfastness, his taste for the absolute, his strictness – everything would all at once fall apart and become embarrassing, cruel and indecent, like an old whore's heavy make-up in the glare

[172]

of the sun. And Jerome's reactions wouldn't be the usual reactions in a man. Alice knew him to be incapable of baseness, incapable of blows or cries, incapable of begging, too. How was he going to respond? What was he going to do?

But it was only when she saw herself standing full-length in the cheval-glass that she realized she had never envisaged any other choice. She had to sleep in Charles's arms that night, and that was that. It was obvious. And how long was it since Alice's desires, impulses, wishes, dislikes had been obvious? Had they ever been? In any case, for once she would go along with them, she would go along with her body and not the maniacal tormentor and tormented thing that was her mind. And though at the same time she hated herself, she closed her eyes and felt she was saved. Saved by the desire these two men had for her – these two males, each of them handsome in his own way – much too handsome for a single scatter-brained woman, whispered a sarcastic voice that she hadn't heard for a long time. After the tragic, raging struggles of her unconscious, here she was playing the heroine in a light comedy. It was a great shame this was taking place in wartime, when everyone was getting themselves killed, and killing each other, when no one would have thought of killing anybody over a woman. At least, she hoped not. And she was seized anew with a fit of silent laughter that came upon her inopportunely and against her will. She imagined Charles and Jerome taking down from the walls the old cavalry sabres that belonged to some grandfather killed at Reichshoffen, and fighting in the moonlight, in white shirts, while she stood at the window, abstracted and distant, applauding the best thrusts and deciding right at the very end to go and sob over the dying man's body, before throwing her arms round the vanquisher's neck.

But what had come over her? For she hadn't yet had

anything to drink; so what were these bubbles leaping to her head, making her as happy as a lark. Had there really been a frustrated, unsatisfied female inside her for the past two years; a female awaiting a male and a slightly better executed embrace in order to rediscover her vitality and happiness? Life, happiness, equilibrium – were the foundations of these so simple? The existence of God, the reason for life – was all this just a matter of glands? She didn't know, but then she didn't care, as long as her glands and her psyche were working. Everything was fine, happiness was for ever innocent, as she had always known it to be; and it was exactly this that had caused her such deep despair when she had lost it. The only unpardonable thing on this earth was unhappiness. And as far as unhappiness was concerned, Jerome was the one who was going to shoulder it, not her any more. He had nursed her, and by way of thanks she had given him her illness, her dreadful illness. At least, she said to herself with sincere cruelty, at least he'll know why he's suffering, and who's causing him to suffer; and contrary to what he thinks when the time comes, this will be a great advantage.

She went into the drawing room and stopped on the threshold. Jerome was lying on his favourite divan, which was covered in a threadbare material that must have once had a design of Louis-Philippe flowers on it, flowers already faded to start with. His cigarette was hanging down from his long hand, at the end of his arm, but already there were dozens of photographic negatives coming between Jerome's face and the pupils of her eyes. Jerome at Spa, at Bayreuth, Jerome leaning over her in that clinic, Jerome on deck clasping Gerhardt's shoulders, Jerome astonished and dazzled in the hotel bedroom in Vienna, Jerome being decisive and sure of himself in the company of others, Jerome stammering in

[174]

front of her. These images passed rapidly before her eyes, just like the pages of a calendar scattering in the wind to indicate the passage of time in bad films; and the images blurred the face that had for so long been her only refuge, her only shore; the face that, she knew, regarded her own face as the only face in the world.

How was she going to say those things, do those things? Shame, anger with herself and despair stifled her and brought tears to her eyes. Jerome misinterpreted this, sat up and, leaning towards her, took her in his arms. She sank into his embrace, resting against Jerome's body as she had done a hundred times, a thousand times before, with her eyes closed on his shoulder and breathing in that smell of eau de Cologne that was so familiar to her and, alas, such a brotherly smell. He was wearing the little red and white scarf she had bought him at Charvet's in those last days when you could still buy little silk scarves; the little red and white scarf that he was never without, that he had never lost, that was more precious to him than the rest of his wardrobe put together; a little scarf that in itself summed up all the hidden romanticism, all the passion and taste for the absolute that this man possessed.

'Jerome,' she moaned, with her eyes closed. 'Jerome, I'm so sad, Jerome!'

He had raised his chin a little, she could feel his cheek, scarcely rough at all, against her own, and his usual warmth, and as she felt his jaws moving against her own cheeks, at the same time she heard him say, 'I know, Alice, I know. I know that you loved them too. You didn't know them, but, you know, they adored you. They thought you were very beautiful, they envied me, they used to say that I was a lucky devil. Me, a lucky devil!' he said with a little laugh. 'I'd never thought of myself as a lucky devil before then. But with you, Alice, yes, I am a lucky devil.'

[175]

'Jerome,' she said in a low, hurried voice, 'Jerome, listen to me.'

'I was so lonely without you,' he went on. She could still feel the inexorable movement of his jaw against her cheek, the movement of his whole head, which didn't want to understand, or imagine, or endure what she was going to tell him.

'I was so lonely, and I was so frightened for you, you can't imagine how frightened I was. I haven't even kissed you. I haven't kissed you, not once, since you got back! And I dreamt about you for three days, four days, I don't know . . . for a hundred years . . .'

And he tipped back Alice's face, apparently not surprised to see long, warm tears flowing down it freely; insistent, urgent tears that streamed down her chin, her neck, her blouse; tears that were literally spurting from her closed eyes. And without even questioning her, he bowed over this ravaged face and placed his mouth on hers, which tightened, closed, then suddenly opened in a kind of sob that for once he didn't react to.

It was then that Charles came in and, as in some 1900 vaudeville act, saw them entwined in each other's arms, kissing. It was then, still as in some vaudeville act, but from the stone age this time, that he beat his chest with his fist, and with a raucous howl, sending everything flying across the room, he rushed at Jerome and literally tore him away from Alice. She was still leaning backwards and let herself sink onto the sofa without a word or a cry, with her eyes closed and both arms clasped round her head, not wanting to see anything, or know anything, or hear anything. Having rolled to the ground, the two men slowly got to their feet and stood facing each other, feeling stupid and contrite and, for once, truly fellow men. Two men out of caves, Jerome thought for one second, very rapidly, before the mad, pathetic

[176]

hope that Alice might still belong to him, and to him alone, flickered and died.

'But you're mad,' he said to Charles, 'but you're mad. What's got into you?'

'You've no right, no right to do that, she's mine,' said Charles.

He was red beneath his suntan, he was sweating; and finally he lashed out in a harsh, violent voice, 'She's mine, you've got no right to touch her! Mine, do you hear? Mine, Jerome.'

Then he stood immobile, cast a rapid glance at Alice, who continued to hide behind her arms, then at Jerome, who also remained where he stood, all three of them transfixed in grotesque or panic-stricken attitudes like the unfortunate inhabitants of Pompeii.

'What do you mean?' said Jerome. 'Alice? Alice, what does he mean?'

'I'll explain,' she said. She slowly brought both arms down, slipping them from her head to her knees with a gracefulness both men unconsciously registered.

'Alice,' asked Charles, 'Alice, he didn't hurt you?'

And she smiled. She smiled at that confidence of his that was as crazy as it was boundless; as though from the moment he loved a woman, Charles was incapable of imagining that she might be unfaithful to him unless she was forced to be.

'No,' she said, shaking her head, 'no, he didn't hurt me. Not at all. Please, Charles, leave us. I must talk to Jerome.'

'Wait,' said Jerome, as Charles made for the door. And he went towards him, his arms dangling. 'Bastard,' he hissed, 'little bastard. You shit. You've never been anything else, have you? A thief, a womanizer, a fraud. And a coward as well! You bastard!'

Charles's head turned to right and left, as though he was being struck. His eyes were closed and he remained

[177]

silent. It was only when Jerome fell silent that he did an almost military about-turn and strode out of the room.

Chapter Fifteen

ALICE HAD instinctively got to her feet when Jerome advanced on Charles, and she remained standing until he left. Jerome was now facing her, and the space that separated them, their melodramatic poses and the banality of their drama pained them both. It was the first time Alice had seen Jerome in a role unworthy of him, and it was her own fault. She was in despair. She wanted to take in her arms this little boy who was so old for his years, so serious, so responsible and so vulnerable. What was she going to say to him? He wasn't hard enough to abuse her nor stupid enough to blame her. He said nothing. He watched her with scared attentiveness, with a feverish lack of understanding.

'Forgive me,' he said at last in a voice that sounded distorted, even deeper than usual – for Jerome could have been a baritone – 'forgive me, Alice, I'd like to sit down. It's all so painful . . .'

He made a vague gesture that took in the drawing room, where the great lost love of his life was seated, and also the outside world beyond the window, where the corpses were piling up.

So little room . . . thought Alice, we actually take up so little room on this great globe as our lives ravel and unravel. Standing, we must occupy a sliver of space, like some broken lamp-post, like a cylinder with, let's say, a radius of eighty centimetres and a height of one or two metres. Then, we're laid out flat, and it's the opposite. If our bodies didn't decompose there would surely be complete layers upon layers of dead men and women, all round the Earth. An Earth entirely encircled, girded, strewn with corpses, with successive layers of corpses . . . how was one to know?

These were the kind of rambling thoughts that she liked to heap on Jerome, who always found some morality in them, some poetry, or some sort of humour. Charles would rely on humour; or else, with pencil in hand, he would devote himself to crazy multiplications that would allow him to announce proudly that the Earth's circumference would then measure an extra metre. But what was she thinking of? What were these stupid questions running round inside her head, when right here in front of her Jerome was suffering because of her, and even she was holding back the tears? What was this insensitive, irresistible little beast that turned up inside her brain every now and then, and took control? 'Listen, Alice,' Jerome was saying, gazing into an imaginary fire in the hearth – fortunately, it was imaginary, for even with all the blinds down and evening coming on, she could still hear the heat thrumming on the terrace, and a silent conflagration moving stealthily through the grass.

'Listen,' Jerome was saying, 'please tell me what happened, in the order it happened.'

'Well, Charles's account was accurate,' she said, speaking too in a low voice, as though there were microphones all round the room. 'It was six o'clock, I think, when we came out of the *Kommandantur*. We found a carriage – by some miracle, because it must have been late. It was fine, though,' she said thoughtlessly.

And something spellbound in her voice suggested it

all to Jerome: an empty Paris, a spring dawn, the sound of a horse's hoofs on the cobblestones, the somnolent Seine, Paris offered up to them, and their weariness, relief and complicity. He put his hand to his face, but with the palm extended and turned outwards, towards her, as though to take the brunt of her blows. Only he would have done better to turn that palm to his chest. For it was his imagination and memory and heart that were fuelling his anguish. Alice saw that hand of his interposed between Jerome and herself, the hand that had for so long and for such long periods held and warmed her own, that for three years had been open and offered to her. The memory of the warm, firm touch, the slightly bony feel of that hand was suddenly so distinct to Alice's own hand that she drew her knees up and clasped her arms round them in a huddle. Someone inside her was crying, 'Jerome, Jerome, help!' Someone who wasn't herself any more, but a child, a meek delicate child, a delightful child perhaps, but one she must now forsake.

'And then?' said Jerome.

'And then – Charles didn't tell you but there was a big scene, a dismal scene at the *Kommandantur*. The officer talked about my taste for Jews, for circumcised men. Charles rushed at them, and they beat him senseless. When he came to, they wanted to check whether or not he was Jewish . . . or at least, make me check . . . They tore his trousers off him, and poor Charles stood there in front of me, in nakedness and shame, in his dinner jacket and socks. To comfort him, I made a point of looking impressed instead of prudish. I almost whistled in admiration. But he was humiliated, dreadfully humiliated. And when we got back to the hotel . . .'

'If I understand you correctly, you went along with it out of compassion?'

'No!' Alice's voice was sharp. It was the voice of anger,

a voice she rarely used and one that Jerome instantly recognized. But he lacked all caution.

'No, I didn't just go along with it. I enticed him into it myself, I drew him to my bed myself; for I found him enormously attractive.' She stopped. 'Jerome, don't make me say these things.'

'I'm sorry,' said Jerome abstractedly.

He could hear his heart beating, with dull regular beats, so loud that they deafened him; the noise was infernal. Oh! If only he could die now, this minute, right here! And never again see, never again dream of that lovely face, that ravaged guilty face before him. The face he had never seen distorted, convulsed, transformed by sexual pleasure. Oh! if only he were able no longer to hear that voice – slightly husky, but so light – neither to listen to it, nor dangle from it! The voice he had never heard sounding breathless or violent, shrill or throaty, either; the voice he had never heard sounding broken, or hungry, or exhausted, or satisfied! The voice he had never heard cry out his own name – 'Jerome, Jerome!' – in the innermost sanctum of a bed. The voice that had perhaps cried out 'Charles!' the day before.

Why? How? He felt capable of seizing Charles by the throat, of putting a knife to his heart and asking for every detail, every particular, every practical exercise of this pleasure he himself had not been able to offer Alice. His baseness overwhelmed him, but he was utterly subject to his obsession.

'Are you thinking of staying here with him?'

'Yes, Jerome,' said Alice.

The tears sprang to her eyes again and trickled down her cheeks, for this 'yes' had an irreversible, official, definitive ring to it. By this 'yes' she solemnized something shameful and ephemeral; by this 'yes' she tore apart and lost this man who was the person closest to her, who had been her sole bulwark against loneliness

[182]

and madness. For she was mad, yes, she was mad, she'd gone crazy! How could she live without Jerome? But how? And if she had a nightmare, if she wanted to talk about it and free herself from this nightmare, from her fantasies, from her terrors, who could she turn to, who would be able to understand her, or would want to? What lover, even if he was crazy about her body, would put up with her mind? Her foolishness was dizzying and deadly. She had lost all reason. She remembered her past with Jerome, she imagined their future.

But as she went through these images in her mind, as though they were arguments that would take her back to Jerome, a particular memory of him came to the fore: Jerome standing in a doorway, with the door half-open, in that horrible clinic in the mountains, Jerome, who'd come to fetch her . . . and another image, an imaginary one this time, of a cocktail party on a terrace, and the two of them, Jerome and herself, leaning back on the balcony, watching people pass by with little ironic smiles, both of them with the same smile. But then between these two images an absurd image had slipped in, an image of Charles asleep, mumbling reassurance, and in the end settling on her shoulder like a gigantic babe-in-arms; from this very safe place he would now and then give her a comforting little pat on her hair and fall onto her nose or her cheek, each time this happened wresting her from incipient sleep. Of course, this image was less comforting than the others, the previous ones – but in its favour was the fact that it was in colour.

'Alice,' said Jerome, speaking suddenly more sharply, 'Alice, you won't stay long with Charles. It's the war that has brought you together, you're not the same kind of people, or from the same background, or even from the same world, morally speaking. When I talk of background, I'm not criticizing Charles; on the contrary, I find his background more reliable than yours. But Alice, he . . . I don't know . . . but you and him – it's so strange. What are you going to talk to him about? What is he going to say in reply? What do you see in him?'

He looked so serious, so anguished in his perplexity that Alice felt like laughing.

'What do I see in him . . . I see in him everything that you see in him yourself, Jerome, since you've been his best and only friend for the past twenty years. I don't know! Charles is cheerful, he's funny, you're never bored with him, he has a love of life, of people . . . I don't know . . .'

'That's true,' Jerome acknowledged, feeling simultaneously exasperated and interested, 'that's true, you're never bored with him; he's lighthearted because he's empty, I fear. No, Alice, no, you're well aware that what binds you to him is something quite different.'

'Whatever it is, it's something I shall never speak of to anyone else,' she said drily, 'not to you, in any case. Now look, Jerome, just think, what exists between you and me is so important and so rare: tenderness, trust, partnership – just think, Jerome, of all that exists between you and me . . .'

He waved his hand, and this stopped her. She had turned red from the moment Jerome had started on this subject and her face was still red. It's funny, he thought in a final burst of supreme lucidity, she's the one who's ashamed and yet I'm the one who couldn't give her pleasure. She's ashamed, but ashamed of what? Would she be ashamed if she had been affectionately bored with him, as she is with me? No, no, she's ashamed of the pleasure I wasn't able to give her, which he gave her; for it was Charles, good old Charles, the cock-of-the-walk, who had prompted and heard and felt those moans, those words, those gestures of pleasure. Oh no! it was really too horrible, and Jerome raised his face to Alice, a face that had grown smooth and calm with

[184]

despair, a face such as she had already seen twice before, and one that she immediately recognized. The first time it had been inside a coffin, ten years ago, and the second time it was in her own mirror, two years ago.

'Jerome,' she cried out in a choking voice, for his eyes remained lowered, 'Jerome, what can I do for you?'

'Answer me, Alice, answer me! Did he give you pleasure? Do you feel attracted to him? Do you want him, do you want to touch him? And for him to touch you? Are you obsessed with him the whole time? Did he make you moan? Alice, Alice,' he said more loudly, for she had flinched and almost stood up. 'Alice, you must tell me, I must hear your own voice say so, so that I can have no doubts on the matter. I must be sure that it wasn't that you didn't like . . . at least, didn't . . . Alice, I beg you, I must know that it was me, that it was my fault . . . Alice, be savage, be savage with me, I beg you! If you have any reason to be, of course . . .'

And it was the vague, trembling, very feeble doubt quivering in his last words, much more than his entreaty, that decided Alice.

'Yes,' she said, 'yes, Charles gave me pleasure, very quickly. I thought I was dead to that kind of thing, as you know only too well. Then on that much talked-about evening in Paris, what with the alcohol, the emotions, I . . .'

'I'm not asking you to make excuses,' said Jerome drily, 'I'm asking you to tell me precisely what happened.'

He spoke in a hissing voice that Alice didn't know him to be capable of, a voice that enraged her. This refined, discriminating, sensitive man was asking her to give him details of her lovemaking! Her voice, her own voice, suddenly seemed to her to cut through glass: 'If it's technique you're referring to, talk to Charles, Jerome. And if you want to know, it's true that Charles Sambrat

[185]

pleasured me for one day and two nights, from Tuesday to Thursday. It's true that I whispered and moaned, begged and insisted. There.'

'And you told him?' asked Jerome.

'I don't know. I know that I cried out. I don't remember, but I know because Charles told me. And honestly, what can be more clear than the fact that I'm unclear about it. What can be more telling than the fact that I don't know?'

And of course there was no answer to her question. For Jerome knew nothing any more; except that it was a week to the very day, to the very hour, since they had both arrived at Charles's house, the house he was going to leave, alone, within the next hour.

Chapter Sixteen

THE SUMMER that year, in 1942, was one of the finest our planet has ever known, as though the Earth wanted to calm the violence and panic of men with its beauty and gentleness. Against a boundless sky – which was either a watery or intense blue, depending on the time of day – rose the white suns of the night, suns that were sensitive to the cold, followed at midday by yellow, unseeing suns that were scattered in the evening into slanting pink rays, melting and languid, as though to acclaim the end of long delightful days. But in truth, it was a white, unchanging, fixed sun that watched this planet revolve round it, and saw on this planet some dreadful sights. Bodies and yet more bodies were piling up everywhere; they lay on the ground, set down on soil that more often than not was strange to them. Through its magnifying glass the sun could see hands everywhere, clenching and relaxing – dying hands, well cared-for hands and rough hands, children's hands, artists' hands, women's hands, men's hands, hands with broken nails, sometimes with broken fingers, hands that were already bleeding and closed again one last time before opening for ever, upturned towards the sun. Impotent, blinding, horrified, the sun knew that on its next rotation this mad globe would have other hands, other corpses on display.

The Earth itself was still unaware of what a few stupidly inspired learned men were plotting in distant deserts. And yet, the faithful, tender Earth was devoted to her crazy children – these impassioned, fragile foster children whose flesh she was used to nourishing and sheltering, tirelessly, before receiving their bones (as she had done for century upon century, for epochs and eras that they could have not so much as an inkling of) – and, though perturbed by these scenes of carnage, these storms and battles, she offered to men, perhaps for the last time, perhaps to pacify them – the most brilliant of springs, the hottest of summers, the most russet-coloured of autumns, and the driest of winters. The Earth offered seasons, real seasons, such as there had never been before. But the Earth was soon going to find out that her children, these transitory creatures, had discovered the means not only of dying more quickly on her flanks, but of causing her to die along with them; the means to blow her up and destroy their foster mother, their only friend.

During that time, in the pastoral charm of a corner of France that had still been spared the violence, Alice marvelled at the brown colouring of her lover's body, Alice marvelled at the summer and at the summer's warmth. At lunchtime they would go and bathe in the stream and have a picnic. Then Charles would return to the factory and Alice would go back to the house, dragging her feet. She would read, listen to Charles's records, stroke the dog and the cat, discuss life with the cook, men with the maid and the weather with the gardener; she would sit at the piano, playing half-heartedly; she would sigh and smile, get up, walk across a meadow, pick a bunch of flowers, lie down beneath a tree, forget her flowers, go home and prepare a cocktail – an increasingly peculiar cocktail, with all the restrictions, but one that Charles drank with pleasure, it

[188]

seemed. She would see him returning as fast as he could, with the gravel crunching under his wheels; she would see him leap out of his car and climb the steps; she would see his eyes, his mouth, his hands reaching out towards her, then she would see nothing more in the darkness but the weave of his cotton jacket against her nose. And, if she tipped her head back, the extraordinary rightangle between his shoulder and neck. But she almost never raised her eyes, she would close them; she would remain within the darkness of his embrace, breathing in Charles's smell, the smell of soap and the smell of his skin.

She experienced a feeling of ownership, of possession, a feeling previously unknown to her. One that she had, first of all, never felt before and, secondly, always scorned and rejected, in her respect for the freedom and independence of others. Perhaps this sense of ownership had been awakened in her precisely because of the man's being so free, so independent, so solitary despite his sociability, so little subjugated by life, so isolated finally by his happiness at being alive; because he was so replete, so astute, so accomplished, so stable – the complete opposite of her other lovers, so different from all those men she had known and sometimes loved in return, so far removed from the delicate Gerhardt, the vulnerable Jerome . . . from all the men who were split and torn apart by themselves, who all needed her and would have given everything that she should have need of them. Who all of them in some confused way had asked her to make them suffer so that they could feel they existed. And so none of them had been able to get from her what Charles got from her – Charles, the man who needed her not in order to live but to be happy.

And although her transports of feeling might seem to her to be purely sensual, she was well aware that they hid something else besides, something more tender that in the end she could less well own up to. Something that she would one day rediscover in old age, if she reached old age, something that she would rediscover in the haphazard jumble of her memory, bearing the rare label of passion, of joyful passion.

For in the calm gentle tide of her days, the small, cold, dry voice of reason hardly ever cut in any more to ask her what had become of Gerhardt or Jerome; or, more cruelly still, what she was doing with this man who had read nothing, knew nothing of the things she liked, and didn't always care about the same things as she. But straightaway something – a ray of sunshine or a look from Charles, or the feel of the cat's back against her legs – straightaway something concrete and at the same time dreamlike, something warm and tender would come between her, her past, her future and her conditional moods, something she might have already been able to call happiness if the idea had occurred to her and she'd had the strength to do so.

So that summer Alice and Charles shared a few blessed weeks together. Then came September, and squalls of rain buffeted the house and the countryside. Friends of Charles came to see them. Alice entertained them and was delightful to them. They talked of the Prix Goncourt, a lot; of the theatre, a little; and of politics, not at all. In mid-September, Alice would say to herself every day that she ought to go to town and buy some books; for she'd read everything in the house, and after all, she had to do something during those rather long days when Charles didn't get home until seven o'clock, and the rain prevented her from going out. But she failed to want the books enough to go as far as Grenoble. She failed to find the rain sufficiently tedious to get fed up with it. She failed to stir herself or go any further than her bedroom, the drawing room, the kitchen, the attic, always with the cat and dog following her, for they now clung to her the way animals in legends cling to fairies. She would stroll around the big country house, singing, and would be vaguely surprised whenever she came across herself in a mirror. Life, it seemed to her, could go on like this for ever; and she didn't know whether this was just a possibility, a hope or a threat. And she didn't even seek to know.

And when she received a message telling her that Jerome had been taken prisoner near Paris and was doubtless at that very moment being tortured by the Gestapo, when she decided to leave within the hour, and packed her bags with the cook in tears, she still didn't know. Charles was in Lyons, and therefore couldn't be contacted, so she left him a note.

Alice was a clear-thinking woman and yet, when she turned back on the threshold of the bedroom in which she had been living for the past five months, she looked at it as if she really was going to sleep in that bed, in Charles's arms, two weeks later – just as she had promised in her letter to him. But two months later, Charles still had no news from her.

And two months later, on 11 November 1942, the Germans broke the Vichy Accords and crossed the demarcation line. The whole of France was now occupied territory. On 19 November a Gestapo detachment searched the area round Romans and discovered in the little village of Formoy one Joseph Rosenbaum, foreman in a shoe factory, who was of the Jewish race, and whose family had been living in the region since they settled there in 1854. Despite his employer's protests, they arrested him and sent him to the camp at Auschwitz – but not before they had brutally assaulted his wife and set fire to his home.

A reluctant hero, Charles Sambrat then joined the Resistance.

[191]